North and Central

North and Central

Bob Hartley

Tortoise Books
Chicago

FIRST EDITION, APRIL, 2017

Published in the United States by Tortoise Books

www.tortoisebooks.com

ASIN: B06XX5X886
ISBN-10: 0-9860922-8-2
ISBN-13: 978-0-9860922-8-2

Cover image is in the public domain. Image information as follows: Paik, Kenneth, 1940-2006, Photographer
Record group: Record Group 412: Records of the Environmental Protection Agency, 1944 - 2006
Series: DOCUMERICA: The Environmental Protection Agency's Program to Photographically Document Subjects of Environmental Concern, compiled 1972 – 1977
NAIL Control Number: NWDNS-412-DA-11059

Cover design by Jaime Harris

As always, for Mary

For people like me, there is no order.

- John Lydon, "Problems"

In the 1970s, Zenith Corporation manufactured televisions and employed over 12,000 workers in Chicago.

- Emily Clark and Mark Wilson, The Electronic Encyclopedia of Chicago.

Trembling Under Fingers

I was a balding thirty-five-year-old with a belly and heel spurs. My bar took up a corner at North and Central. It was red brick with glass block windows.

It was a Friday in early December and the Old Style sign was swinging in the wind. I sat banging dents into quarters with a hammer and nail. Bill, the night bartender, had called in sick again. And I'd had to stock and clean the bar because Donald, the afternoon guy, hadn't done shit. All I asked for in bartenders was that they showed up, did most of what they were supposed to, and didn't steal too much. Donald was getting too close to the line. Bill had maybe crossed it. With every whack of the hammer, I imagined I was cracking his skull.

Railroad Bob was passed out in a booth with his dirty hair forming a wooly cloud around his head. His boots were sticking out and dripping mud onto my floor. The Skeletons sat with their shoulders hunched. Their elbows were sunk into the bar and they chain-smoked Chesterfields. They were old and gray. Their skin sagged so much it looked like it'd been draped on them. Like always, they were fucking with each other.

"Buy one," she said.

"With what?" he replied.

"Got some."

"Not enough."

"Enough for one."

"Christ. Think only of yourself."

"Asshole."

"You married me."

"Don't remind me."

The arguing was part real and part con. They gambled. If they kept it up long enough, I'd either buy them one or throw them out. Sometimes it's easier to be a sucker. I had too much to do. I gave them two Buds. "On me," I said. "Shut...the...fuck...up."

It was like giving a baby a bottle. They went back to smoking and I went back to work. I'd just started bashing Washington's head again when Rita came in. She always wore this old brown leather bomber jacket with the collar turned up. Her hair was tied back in a ponytail and she had this little gap between her two front teeth. She had these hazel eyes that pierced right through me and made me sometimes forget what I was saying. She hopped onto the stool next to me.

"Seen him?" she asked.

I'd seen Jerry around six and he'd said he'd be in. He told her he'd be working. Jerry lied to her all the time even when the truth was just as good.

Anybody else, I could look straight in the face and lie to, but not her. I looked at the quarters. "No," I said.

She leaned closer and tried to make eye contact. I kept banging dents.

"Really?" she said.

"Really," I said.

"Every payday the asshole's a ghost."

"I can let ya have fifty."

"That's okay."

She leaned even closer. Her arm brushed against mine and the feeling of her skin, even for those few seconds, made me want to take hold of her.

"What are you doin'?" she said.

"Bill called in sick. And on top of that, I'm pretty sure the fucker's been ripping off the jukebox during the week," I said. "I think he's stupid enough to use the register to cash in the quarters. Monday night, when I'm countin' the drawer, if these are there, I'll fire his ass."

She tilted her head a little, laughed, and said I was smart. And because it was her that said it, I believed I was. She told me that, if I saw Jerry, to call her. She hopped off the stool, backed up, and turned toward the door.

Railroad Bob had pulled himself up. He was smoking a cigarette and staring at the table like it was telling him a secret. He looked up and, when he saw her, he smiled and raised a hand that shook a little.

"How's it goin', sister," he said.

"Good," she said. "How's your ma?"

"Dead."

Rita's face went a bit pale. She didn't say anything, but she didn't move either. She needed an out.

"Could be worse," I said. "Right, Bob."

"Yeah," Bob said. "Bitch could still be here."

Rita looked at me and smiled. Then she laughed a little, moved to the door, gave it a pull, and walked out. Railroad Bob got up and threw a five on the bar. I cracked open an Old Style, shoved it in front of him, and made his change. He took a drink and looked over at Old Man Skeleton and said: "Some dead are more alive than the livin'."

"Shut up," Old Man Skeleton said. "Christ, you're a dark bastard."

"Death smiles at me. I smile back."

"Shut the hell up."

I thought about running after Rita and telling her that Jerry had lied and that, if she came back later, she'd find him spending the money she needed. But I couldn't tell her that, because if I had, she'd have known for sure that I was a liar too.

◇◇◇

It started getting busy around eleven.

First, the cops started filing through the back door. On Friday nights there were always three or four squads parked in my alley with the windows rolled down. The cops took turns sitting out back and listening for calls. Most of the time, there were more of them in my bar than they had at roll call. Jerry wasn't on duty. The rest were. They threw their uniform jackets over the barstools and their caps on the bar, then pulled out their shirttails and rolled up their sleeves.

I opened a dozen Old Styles, put them on the bar, and started their tab. They played liar's poker. Each one kept a beer in one hand and a folded dollar bill in the other. They huddled around taking peeks, and making bets. Soon there was a small mountain of crumpled bills piling up on the bar.

The Zenith factory second-shift guys came next. Like the cops, they marked their territory and took up space close to the door. They threw their work coats into a booth, sat down on stools, and cranked their heads to watch the TV. Over the past couple of years, there'd been steady layoffs. So there were fewer of them, but they knew how to drink, and still made up a good part of the business. They ordered pitchers and shots and threw quarters into the Wurlitzer. They loved "Iron Man" and played it over and over.

Finally, I couldn't take it anymore and hit the reset button. When the music stopped, Railroad Bob still stood in front of the box, stomping in place, whipping his hair around with his eyes fixed on the ceiling. He looked like a drunk Jesus waiting for the ascension.

"Bob, the fucking song's over," I said.

But he kept it up. "Fuck you. I'm Iron Man."

"Well look at your pants. Somebody pissed on Iron Man."

Only then did he notice the stain on his crotch. "Mother of mercy," he said. "Is this the end of Bob?" The cops and Zeniths laughed, and somebody bought him a beer.

After a few rounds, the two groups blurred. A few of them started making bets on the Shuffle Alley machine. The puck banged against the pins and each time somebody hit a strike, bells rang, and Catwoman's tits lit up.

Business had been shit and I needed a good night, but I wished they'd stop coming through the door for a while. Still, each time it squeaked meant money. I banged on the register, threw bottles into garbage cans, dumped ashtrays, and wiped up spills. And every ten minutes or so, two or three red or blue flannel shirts walked out the backdoor and came back with slits for eyes, and smelling like weed. The cops paid no heed.

When Gin and Tonic Doc came in, I knew it was midnight. He took his usual spot in the middle of the bar and a few stools from the Skeletons. He sat with his back straight and eyes forward. He kept his ashtray, cigarettes, lighter, coaster and drink in one straight line. He spent most of his time reading some book and waiting for his chance with rough trade.

Then the St. Anne's nurses came in wearing tight sweaters and tighter jeans. Most were from the neighborhood and were friends, sisters, or cousins of the Zeniths and cops. Like the guys, they mostly drank beer. Only tonight there was a new one who looked like one of those big-headed kid paintings that everybody had in the Sixties: frizzy hair, saucer eyes, and puckered lips. She came up to the bar and said: "Make me something special."

"Like what?" I said.

"I don't know. Surprise me."

Christ, I hated people who couldn't make up their minds. It doesn't matter if it comes in a glass or a bottle, it's all fucking alcohol. I surprised her with a shot and an Old Style chaser. "Try Railroad Bob if you want special."

Then this young black guy came in hustling Craftsman knockoff tool sets for twenty bucks. A few suckers were drunk enough to take the bait. He stuck around and bought a beer. One of the nurses smiled at him and said he was cute. He smiled back and said she was cute too. Then he put his arm around her shoulder. People started to stare. I told him it wasn't a good idea. He caught the fierceness of the eyes on him. He took his arm away, gulped down his beer, and left.

When it hit 2:00, we got the swing shift stragglers, and the professional drinkers who'd closed the other neighborhood bars.

It didn't matter how drunk they got. Everyone knew when closing was coming. With two hours to go, even with shots and full beers in front of them, they ordered backups for themselves and each other. And they constantly needed change for the juke box, the pool table, or the cigarette machine. The bastards kept me running from one end of the bar to the other.

Then some asshole came in with a handful of cigars. He handed them out, and soon one end of the bar was covered in a gray cloud. With that and the cigarettes, my lungs were leather.

My back ached more and more the deeper I had to reach into the cooler for a beer. But they kept buying each other drinks. And the Skeletons wouldn't stop singing "When the moon hits your eye like a big pizza pie, that's amoré," even though neither of them could sing worth a good goddamn.

"You're off key," I said. "Shut up."

"You're stiflin' our creativity," Old Man Skeleton said.

"Needs stiflin'."

Then some started plinking away on the upright piano. I don't know why, but, when people get drunk, the bastards think they're Mozart or something. I usually put up with it, but one of the morons started banging on the keys with his fists. I told him to stop or get the hell out.

Then a couple of the cops started shoving each other over a bet. I told Jerry to control his friends. Jerry grinned, shrugged, and told them they should ease up. "It's just a fucking game," he said.

Then some asshole put on that same goddamn disco song from that same shitty goddamn movie that'd been played in every fucking bar for months. Railroad Bob stood in front of the box, gave it the finger, and screamed, "You are the shitstain on American music." The longer it played, the more they shouted that it must have been a nurse that put it on, because nobody else would play that faggot crap. And the nurses said that was bullshit, except for Saucer Eyes, who was now blasted and hanging all over Jerry. And I almost hit the button again, but somebody bumped the Wurlitzer and it reset and we all cheered.

Finally, it was 3:30 and I yelled, "Last call, fellas. Dancing girls waitin' outside."

Somebody by the pool table yelled, "Go fuck yourself."

"If I could," I said, "life'd be easier."

In between final drinks, I threw six packs into paper bags and stuffed the cash into the register. One of the cops pulled his squad in front of the place and threw on the rollers, lighting the place up with flashes of blue. And I yelled, "Squads are out, boys. Squads are out."

A few of them said I was an asshole. Then more joined in and they all started chanting and it got louder and louder until the whole place was screaming: "Andy is an asshole. Andy is an asshole. Andy is an asshole."

I shoved six-pack bags at them.

Jerry had his arm around Saucer Eyes. Her hair looked like a fright wig and there was a smudge of lipstick spread across her cheek.

"Hey, Jerry," I said. "Who's your favorite clown?"

"What?"

"Nothin'."

As they walked toward the door, she stuck her tongue in his ear. He gave me a wink and left with his hand shoved in her back pocket and squeezing her ass. It pissed me off, because, just a few hours before, I'd had to lie for him. I always had to lie for the fucker and there was no payoff.

I poured quick last call shots and blasted them with the bar lights. And they all shouted, "Oh shit." They squinted and clutched damp brown paper bags. And when the Skeletons were making their way to the door, the old man reached his boney arms over the bar and tried to pour himself a Budweiser. I grabbed the glass from his hand and told him to behave himself.

"Why?" he asked.

The Skeletons snapped at each other as I nudged them toward the door.

"Cheap bastard."

"You married me."

"Don't fucking remind me."

I grabbed Railroad Bob by an arm, pulled him out of the booth, got him to his feet, and put his coat on him. For a second, I thought he wasn't going to make it, but then he started moving and I got him into the street. I let go of him. He stood there swaying and staring up at a street light.

"I stare into the hole and it keeps lookin' back," he said.

"Gonna make it home?" I asked.

He looked at me, grinned, and said, "Every pleasure has its price, gherkin."

"Careful," I said. "Gettin' crazy around here."

"We're all a little crazy," he said. Then he took a few steps, put his palms against a brick wall, bent over, and threw up on my neighbor's building. I thought about helping him, but the cold made me walk back in. He wasn't my problem anymore. I pulled hard on the door and locked up.

Bottles, glasses, and dirty ashtrays were all over the bar and booths. A layer of beer mixed with mud and cigarette butts covered the floor. The bar mats were sticky and the coolers were nearly empty. And even though business was down and I'd thought about not replacing the thief, I knew I couldn't handle another Friday night working alone.

As I walked down to the end of the bar, I pulled the stools out. Toward the end, there was a purse. I picked it up and opened it. There was a wallet. Inside it were two twenties and a ten. I took a twenty as a finder's fee. Then I put the wallet back in the purse and put it behind the bar for safekeeping.

It was 6:00 before I finished cleaning and stocking. I always did the books last. Next to the register, I kept a piece of paper with two columns of hash marks—one for six packs and the other for drinks. I pulled the bank and counted the difference. I kept three .38s hidden: one at each end of the bar and another behind the register. I never left them there. There'd been a lot more burglaries lately, and the last thing I needed was to be shot with my own gun. I put two in a plastic bag and one in my pocket. I put the night's take and the list in a bank pouch, grabbed the gun bag, and went down to the basement.

The safe was toward the front of building close to the old coal chute. Next to it was a card table with a few folding chairs around it. On top of it was a long-sleeved flannel shirt and a pair of gardening gloves.

The safe was in the floor. Years before, the place was burglarized and they'd taken the old one. My mother thought it was so heavy no one would be able to get it up the stairs and out the door. She was wrong. So she'd had the basement floor broken up and a safe dropped into it. She said that if the fuckers wanted it, they'd have to bring a jackhammer.

I opened the safe, pulled out the IRS ledger, and put it on the table. Then I put on the shirt and gardening gloves and opened the old coal chute door. Inside was a big pile of black chunks and dust. I pushed my hand into the pile until my arm was covered with coal and I felt the plastic bag. I grabbed and pulled. Inside the bag was the second ledger—the real one.

I took it out of the bag and threw it on the table. I took off the gloves and shirt. I sat down and added up the six-pack money and then the drinks. I took it from the pouch, wrapped the wad with a rubber band and stuffed it into my pocket. I ripped up the lists into small pieces and put them in my pocket too. I always flushed anything that could be used against me. Then I counted the rest and entered the total into the IRS book.

I put the cash in a deposit envelope, licked it, sealed it, and put it back into the pouch. I closed the book, opened the other, and entered the total amount of Saturday's take.

On the inside flap of the book was a pocket with some envelopes. I spread them out. Under each flap was written 100, 50, 20, or 10. I never wrote anything else on the envelopes. I didn't need names. It was 1978, it was Chicago, and it was Austin. Everybody, from the local juice loan guy to the neighborhood priest, knew the way the game was played. And even though the bar wasn't making near what it used to, I still had to pay the fuckers their money.

One hundred went to Jerry who bumped it up to his district commander. Fifty went to the liquor control people. Twenty went to fire, health, building or any other inspector who might come by looking for some trumped up violation. Ten went to random cops for hauling away drunks or bouncing the occasional asshole.

But I rarely had anybody busted. My mother taught me that anybody can have a few too many and have a bad night. Unless they were always causing trouble, you wanted them to come back. They can't spend their money if they're in jail.

I filled any empty envelope and put them back into the ledger's pocket. I put the pouch and IRS book back into the safe and closed it.

Austin Federal had a drop box, but I never made a deposit at the same time or on the same day. Sometimes, I'd even skip a week. I was taught that, in the bar business, especially in a neighborhood like mine, I should expect to get robbed once or twice, but that didn't mean I had to make it easy for the bastards.

I put the gloves and flannel back on, took the real ledger, put it back into its plastic bag, and shoved it deep into the pile of coal. I did the same with the gun bag. I shut the chute door, took off the gloves and shirt, and went upstairs to wait for Donald.

At 6:45, Donald pounded on the door. He was big and looked tough. He even had a tattoo of an eagle on his skull. He was harmless. It's usually the little psychopaths that are the most dangerous. They'll slit your throat just for being in the same room with them. But Donald's size and that tattoo kept me from having any trouble during the day. Plus, again, he showed up, and he didn't steal too much.

I unlocked the door, we traded nods, and I walked out. I made sure the tavern never opened earlier or closed later than the license allowed. Still, there was a small group of Zenith night shifters and early morning drunks huddled around the front of the bar shifting feet and blowing into fists. And, even though it had never happened before, they all looked at me like this was the morning I'd let them in early. That hungry look is what hustlers depend on.

It reminded me of being a kid waiting for the fucking nuns to open the school doors in January. On those days, it didn't matter that my mother had wrapped me up in my winter coat, scarf, and hat, and that she'd put my feet in plastic bags and covered them with my socks and shoes. It didn't matter that I kept my hands balled up inside my gloves all the way to St. Lucy's. The cold still cut through my pants, stung my face, and numbed my fingers. The snow still managed to get past the plastic bags. By the time I got to school, my feet were frozen stubs.

We stood there in straight lines. We huddled together, stomped our feet, and hunched our shoulders. We looked like little slaves in a gulag. But even for the littlest ones, the nuns would still never open up early. They would just stand inside and make small talk until the bell rang and, then, finally, they'd unlock the damn doors and let us in for another day of getting smacked around.

Even before the school day started, they made sure we knew who was in charge. How anybody can say they liked those bitches is beyond me. I never met one I didn't want to shove in front of a train.

When the drunks heard the click of Donald locking the door, they looked at me the way I looked at those nuns. I knew what they needed, but wouldn't give it to them. Instead, I just shrugged, shoved my hands in my pockets, and kept moving. I'm sure they wanted to shove me in front of a train too.

I'd always lived above the bar. First with my parents and then alone. It was just cold enough to make me fumble the keys and drop them. I picked them up, slipped the key in the lock, and gave the door a shove. I grabbed the Trib lying against the hallway door. I unlocked the door and looked up at the stairs. It wasn't a long way, but after working twelve hours, it didn't matter. I stalled. I unwrapped the paper, sat on the steps, and read until I caught myself nodding off. I dropped the paper, pulled myself up, and made the climb. Then I ate a quick bowl of cereal and went to sleep on the couch.

West Side Youth Guilty of Boy's Murder

By James Thompson

SIXTEEN-YEAR-OLD Ezekiel Thomas was found guilty on Tuesday of murdering ten-year-old William Fisher.

On July 19, 1978, Thomas and his accomplice, fifteen-year-old Jeremiah Woodson, were allegedly burglarizing Fisher's home when they discovered Fisher hiding under his bed. The boy was home playing hooky from school. According to prosecutors, when Fisher recognized him as an acquaintance of his older brother, Thomas decided to murder the boy.

Pivotal in Thomas's conviction was the cooperation and testimony of Woodson. He testified that, after tying the boy's hands, they forced him into Thomas's car.

"First, we went to [Thomas's] girl's house, 'cause we were gonna OD him," Woodson stated.

When it was discovered that the girl didn't have enough drugs to successfully "OD" the boy, Fisher was forced back into the car and driven to the Thatcher Woods Forest Preserve. The boy was then marched deep into the woods where authorities say Thomas stabbed him at least twenty times.

According to Woodson, Thomas was surprised at how difficult it was to kill the boy. "Zeke had this short knife and had to keep stabbing him. The kid kept saying, 'Ya said it'd be quick, Zeke.'"

When asked if Thomas said anything in reply, Woodson stated, "Yeah. He said it wasn't like TV."

For his cooperation, Woodson pled guilty to voluntary manslaughter and was sentenced to fifteen years. Thomas's sentencing hearing is set for February 9, 1979.

No Teeth—No Drinks

Every Wednesday night I went to Jerry and Rita's. Jerry sat at one end of the table playing daddy. He wore a small crucifix around his neck. It always amazed me how, every Sunday, most of the cops I knew could kneel down next to the same people they ripped off the rest of the week. But, then again, most of the other churchgoers were doing the same thing.

He had a pilsner glass in front of him with a crumpled Old Style can next to it. He wore dirty sneakers, an old pair of jeans, and a striped Cubs jersey. But even without his uniform, he couldn't help but look like a cop. He had this bushy mustache and sideburns that they all seemed to have back then, but it was more than that. He drank his beer, told corny jokes to his kids, and talked sports with me. But, every once in a while, he'd flash me this get-me-the-fuck-out-of-here look. Even on his day off, in his own house with his wife and kids and best friend, he could never let the streets go.

Rita sat opposite Jerry. She was leaning back and fiddling with a fork. She wore a black sweater with matching jeans. Her hair was down and it covered her shoulders. Around her neck, on a silver chain, she wore the Claddagh ring I'd given her when we were in high school. She didn't always wear it, and I remember wondering why she was wearing it that night.

I sat across from the kids, like the pitiful uncle who'd never married.

Every once in a while, people asked me about going into the bar business. I always told them that, if they wanted friends, to choose something else. I learned early on that it was people who said they were your friends that did the most sponging. Besides employees, they're the ones who'll make you go broke, and when you do, they're nowhere to be found. My only friends were Jerry and Rita.

Rita never let money get in the way of setting a good table. What she didn't make herself, she found in junk stores. She said most people didn't know the beauty they could find right in front of them. The table was covered with an embroidered tablecloth. In the center of it, she'd sewn the trunk of a tree surrounded by little grass patches. A series of branches arched from the trunk and became smaller and smaller until they ended in tiny emerald green leaves. The leaves became a chain that created a border. For each place setting, she used china plates with red, blue, and yellow flowers. There were white linen napkins, and polished silverware. In the middle of the table was a glass vase. In it was a tree she'd made from branches found in the backyard. Dinner was just meatloaf, potatoes, gravy, and broccoli, but, because of what she'd done with that table, for a little while, I felt like I was in a place far from the neighborhood.

I liked watching her with her kids. The boy was eight and the girl ten. The boy was staring at the girl's plate. He asked why his sister had more food than he did.

"We like her more," Rita said, and even though it was a running gag, it made me laugh. "After dinner, she gets a pony."

The boy looked hurt, until she leaned over, kissed him, pointed to his plate and said, "You never finish."

The boy grinned. Rita told him his sister was still getting the pony. Then she told them to get their jackets and go outside. And they moaned that they didn't want to.

"How long?" the girl asked.

"When ya can't feel your feet, come in," Rita said. Then she pointed toward the back door and, with slits for eyes and gritted teeth, she said, "Go."

They put on their coats and hats and trotted toward the door. As they walked out, Jerry hollered, "Write if ya get work."

It was another running gag, but it didn't make me laugh. It was just one more thing he forced. If I hadn't watched Rita struggle, if he'd been a real father to them, maybe I would've. He was my best friend, but that didn't mean I had to like him.

I thought it was strange that she sent them away. We usually played some board game or cards. The boy was really good at blackjack. Most of the time, he took me for a few bucks. "What's goin' on?" I said.

Rita traded looks with Jerry. She took a second and then said, "How'd it go with that bartender?"

I told her I'd fired him.

She asked if I'd be hiring somebody. I told her I would. She put her fork down, leaned to me, and said, "Jimmy needs work."

Jimmy "Fatboy" Tracey, Rita's younger brother, was a junkie. A drooling, shaking, itching, stealing, lying, motherfucking junkie. And possibly a murderer, too. The best thing for everybody was when he finally got locked up.

"Yeah?" I said.

"He's clean."

"Just got out."

"No," she said. "He's really different. And he's been out for a while."

She told me that she'd waited to ask me because she wanted to make sure her brother was really off heroin. She told me that Jimmy was doing really well and looked great and that, as soon as he could, their father would get him on at Zenith. And she sounded convincing because, even though Zenith hadn't been hiring for months and everybody was worried about their jobs, she believed it was going to happen. Her father was a union steward and had pull. She said that, as soon as someone retired, he'd get Jimmy a job. She said that her father was a bastard, but not a lying bastard.

"Great," I said.

"But 'til then, he needs work."

She stopped speaking and waited for the words to sink in. I knew I'd give in and so did she, but I didn't answer right away. I couldn't let on that I could be swayed so easily. I needed to fool myself into believing that I didn't love her as much as I did, but the truth was that she had more power over me than anyone I'd ever known.

I knew replacing one thief with a worse one was a really stupid idea, but what bothered me most was that she was letting her brother con her again. Like any junkie, he used her love to feed his arm, and, now, it was like he'd never left. He was just out of prison and already making a sucker out of the person who cared about him most. Asshole.

"You can say no." Jerry said. "I would."

"Shut up, Jerry," she said.

Jerry got up from the table and walked into the kitchen for another beer. "I'm lookin' out for my friend," he said.

She put her hand on my arm. "He needs this," she said.

I nodded and I knew I couldn't say no. I asked her if Jimmy was really clean, and she said that he was, and all he needed was a chance. I told her that I couldn't make any promises, but to have him come around to the tavern on Thursday night and I'd talk with him. But we both knew that, as long as Jimmy looked the part, I'd give him the job.

She sprang up from the table, kissed me on the cheek and hugged me. Her hair brushed against my face, her hands moved down my back, and I trembled under her fingers.

◇◇◇

Jerry gave me a ride back to the tavern. He was supposed to just drop me off, but instead he pulled the car into a spot and came in for a beer. The place was empty except for the Skeletons, Railroad Bob, and Donald.

As soon as he saw us come through the door, Donald grabbed his money from the tip jar and slipped past with a six pack tucked under his arm. I took his place behind the bar. Jerry took a seat close to me. I pulled the bank from the till and counted the remaining cash.

"How much?" Jerry said.

"A hundred," I said.

"Probably rang one ten. Don't know how you work with criminals."

"Ten I can live with. Plus I already had to can one thief."

"Just in time to hire another."

Railroad Bob pulled himself from his booth and ordered a beer. I cracked one open and gave it to him.

"Property is theft, gherkin," he said.

"Uh-huh," I said. "Back to your cave, Bob."

I pulled an Old Style from the cooler, opened it, and put it in front of Jerry. We stared at the Zenith. The Blackhawks and the Rangers were zooming from one end of the rink to the other. The puck was a tiny black blur.

It was the last of the third period and we watched Tony Esposito, the Blackhawk goalie, humiliate his brother Phil, the Rangers center.

I loved the way Tony played. When the Rangers got possession of the puck, he crouched into his butterfly stance and faced his brother. Shot after shot, many of them going one hundred miles an hour, flew at him. He flopped from one side of the net to the other. His stick, gloves, and pads were all over the place. His lack of finesse should have been his weakness, but he stopped everything that came at him.

When his shifts were over, Phil would sit on the bench and stare at his brother. You could see the frustration pouring out of him. Tony just couldn't be rattled, even by family. The Hawks won 3-0.

At the end of the game, Tony didn't stop to talk to anybody, not even Phil. He pulled off his mask, wiped his face with a towel, and skated to the locker room. To the end, he was all business. I envied him.

"You really gonna give Fatboy a job?" Jerry said.

"I guess," I said.

"Gonna rob you blind."

"Time for you to go?"

"Not finished."

"Hurry up."

"Fuck you."

"How come you never go home?"

"It sucks. Mortgage, car, electric, gas, tuition. All she talks about is money. Always. She used to be fun. Remember? No more. It's like being married to a bill collector. It's amazing I go back at all. Christ, sometimes I even wish you'd married her." He gulped down his beer and stood up.

I wanted to tell him it was his fault. He'd made her into a bill collector. I wanted to tell him I wished I'd married her too and that, if he didn't stop fucking around, I'd do my best to take her from him. But I didn't, because I knew I couldn't make good on it.

"So, goin' home then?" I said. He laughed, gave me the finger and walked out.

Railroad Bob's hand rose from his booth. "What am I?" he asked. "A orphan?"

"Legs broke?" I said.

He pulled himself from the booth and walked toward the bar, and said, "All great thoughts come from walkin', gherkin."

"Uh-huh." I gave him another beer. He threw a crumpled bill on the bar. I rang it up and gave him his change. He took a couple gulps and pointed at me.

"All trouble comes from other people," he said.

"Uh huh," I said.

"Shut up," Old Man Skeleton said. "I'm drinkin'."

When Fatboy opened the door, the blast of light and cold made our heads snap.

Back when we were kids, he'd always inhale the chips and candy he'd lifted from the corner stores. So he'd plumped up, and picked up a nickname to match. In the neighborhood, nicknames were never nice, and almost always putdowns. People zeroed in on your weakest point and pecked at it until it scarred over. I used to think it wasn't right, but as I got older, I understood. It prepared you for the world.

But now Fatboy was not fat, and it was clear he was off heroin. Like almost everyone I'd known who'd done time, prison added muscle. He'd tried to dress the part of a bartender—black dress pants and a white long-sleeved shirt. But he wore dirty high tops and an old jean jacket with frayed cuffs and collar. He stopped halfway in and blew on his hands to warm them up, and a gust of wind caught the half-open door. It flew open, and we were treated to a blast of cold air.

The Skeletons were sitting in the middle of the bar. The old man was wearing the gray pinstripe coat he always wore. It was so thin you could see the imprint of his spine. Under his boney ass was an old overcoat. He shivered, squinted and shielded his eyes with one hand. "Shut the fucking door," he said.

Fatboy pulled the door shut. He took his jacket off and put it on a stool. He didn't wait for his eyes to adjust and just walked toward me, staggering like a drunk. He bumped into a couple of stools and stumbled over Railroad Bob's muddy work boots. "Watch it, gherkin," Railroad Bob said.

Fatboy apologized, brushed a smudge of mud off his pants and kept moving. He combed his hair back with his hands. (There are a few ways to tell somebody's been locked up. They open a pack of cigarettes from the bottom and keep it upright in a shirt pocket, they keep a forearm in front of their plate when they eat, and they use their hands to comb their hair.)

Old Lady Skeleton swiveled around on her stool. She took the cigarette from her mouth, and, with a plastic nail, scraped some lipstick from her teeth. She looked him over head to toe as he walked past.

"Pretty boy," she said.

"Shut up," Old Man Skeleton said.

"Somebody's jealous."

"He's a goddamn baby."

"Just 'cause I read the menu, don't mean I'm buyin'."

"Hag."

"Not what you said last night."

"I was drunk."

"Sure, tiger."

I sat at the end of the bar pretending to read the paper. When he got in front of me, I looked up. Christ, up close, he looked like a recruiting poster model for the Waffen SS–blond hair, blue eyes, carved cheeks and chin.

"Where's your armband?" I said.

"What?" he asked.

"What time's the rally?"

"Huh?"

"Nothin'. Come on."

I brought him behind the bar and showed him around. There were two stations with speed racks, ice bins and pop guns. The speed racks were for the house brands and some of the call liquor. The rest of the call and premium liquor was on shelves on the back bar. "Once in a while you'll get some asshole from after a party at the Manor come in and ask for somethin' weird," I said. "But most of the time, it'll be shots and beers."

I showed him the register with the sheet of prices taped to it. The machine was so old that a lot of the numbers had been rubbed off and some of the buttons stuck. (I'd thought about replacing it, but I couldn't. When my parents bought the tavern, it came with it. Like a lot of stuff in the place, it reminded me of them.) I told Fatboy that, until he got to know what the buttons meant, he was going to have to guess and that, if he made a mistake, to make a note and put it in the drawer. "If ya don't," I said, "difference comes outta your pocket.

Above the register, there was a sign, **No Teeth—No Drinks**. "I mean it," I said. "They drool." I showed him the beer coolers. I explained how to stock, and had him wash and put away some glasses. "You need to keep the bar clean and stocked," I said. "I come in and the ashtrays are full, there's tons of dirty glasses, or the coolers are low, we're gonna have a problem."

Finally, I brought him down to the basement and showed him the stockroom. I switched on the light. The fluorescents buzzed and flickered before coming on. On one wall, I kept the cases of Old Style on wood skids. They were piled to the ceiling. On another were the metal shelves with bottles of gin, vodka, whiskey, and scotch. Next to them, were cases of Yoho potato chips. (When I was a kid, while my friends were playing street hockey or softball after school, or sneaking smokes, or fooling with girls, I was filling the ice bins, and stocking the beer coolers and chip racks. I hated it. On each chip bag was a picture of a smiling kid in a sailor suit giving me the thumbs up. I always wanted to slap the smile right off that fat little bastard's face.)

Finally, I showed Fatboy the Old Style and Budweiser barrels. I told him to rock them to see if any needed changing. The Budweiser, the Skeletons' favorite, was empty. (As always, Donald was lazy. He'd served them Old Style and let them think it was Budweiser. I'd done it myself when it was busy, and I wasn't above pouring a short shot on an amateur drinking Bloody Marys or some other idiotic concoction, but days weren't busy, and there was no advantage in conning the Skeletons.) I could have changed it earlier, but I wanted to show Fatboy how it was done. I had him turn off the gas, unhook the empty, and switch it out.

After, we sat at the card table near the safe. On it was a pile of the dented quarters. I told him how I'd caught the thief.

Then, like I did with everybody I hired, I told him a joke about a bar owner who hires a new bartender. The owner shows the bartender around and then tells him he's going in the back to take a nap, but instead he really watches the bartender through a hole in the wall. A customer comes in. The bartender serves him, rings up the sale, and puts the money in the till. The customer orders a second drink. The bartender serves him, but stuffs the money in his pocket. This goes on for a while. The bartender pockets the money every other drink. But then he pockets the money twice in a row. The owner runs out front and yells, *Hey! Aint we partners no more?*

"In the bar business, you're expected to steal," I said. "Anybody says any different is either lyin' or don't know what the hell they're talkin' about. Steal every tenth drink and don't shortchange regulars. Just the ones who come in once in a while. Make sure they're drunk when ya do it." (What I didn't tell him was that I shortchanged regulars all the time. I wasn't stupid about it. I didn't do it to the same drinker every time. I spread it out, but everybody got their turn.)

I pointed at the pile of quarters and said, "Everybody's a thief, but this fucker was greedy."

I handed him his schedule: Wednesday and Thursday during the day and Friday, Saturday, and Sunday nights. I told him to buy regulars every fourth drink and, even though there hadn't really been any new customers for a year, I told him to buy them every third.

"I'll be with you for the first week or two until you get the hang of it," I said. "After that, we'll work together on Friday and Saturday nights. At night, after twelve, don't ring up any of the six packs, but make sure you put the money in the till. Keep track on a piece of paper how many you sell. I'm doin' your sister a favor here. Don't fuck me over. If you do, I'll do my best to fuck you over worse. Understand?"

"Yeah," he said and he looked a little hurt. Junkies, whether they're using or not, are an amazing thing. Even though they'll steal their mother's last nickel, they still get all weepy when you question their integrity.

"You aint gonna get rich," I said, "But you'll pay your bills."

"That's all I need," he said. "Thanks."

"No dope," I said.

"No dope," he said. And he sounded like he meant it, but junkies always sound honest right up until the time you find them on the street selling your TV.

Above us, we heard the squeak of the door. Next thing, the old lady started hollering for a drink. I led the way and we hustled upstairs.

Nobody'd left. Gin and Tonic Doc had come in early and taken up station at the bar. His overcoat was neatly folded on the stool next to him, and he'd spread out the *Trib* in front of him.

The old lady stared at us like a drunk basset hound. Her mouth was open and her tongue was hanging out.

She held an empty glass in a shaking hand. "Is that you, gorgeous?" she asked. "The thirst's made everything so fuckin' blurry. Fill 'er up, baby."

Railroad Bob sat up, raised both hands above his head, and said, "Me too, gherkin. I'm fightin' a hard battle over here."

I handed Fatboy a bar towel, took my seat, and said, "Serve 'em."

West Side Man Killed With Bayonet

By James Thompson

THIRTY-YEAR-OLD Anthony Pedilla was stabbed to death Friday morning.

Mr. Pedilla was commuting to his job at Zenith Radio Corporation when he allegedly encountered Thomas O'Connor of 5760 W. Wabansia.

Mr. O'Connor was double parked and blocking the street. Mrs. O'Connor told police that, when she heard a horn blaring, she thought it was her husband growing impatient.

"When I came out," Mrs. O'Connor said, "I saw Tommy standing in the street with the bayonet. There was blood everywhere."

Police estimate the victim was stabbed at least six times. He was pronounced dead at the scene. Mr. Pedilla was the father of two and had been a Zenith employee for ten years.

O'Connor was arrested and placed in Cook County Jail where he awaits a bond hearing.

Behold, the Dog Breath Experience

After a few weeks, I knew Fatboy could work the bar alone. He'd gotten to know the regulars. They liked him, but he didn't put up with any of their shit. Plus, he was on time, hadn't missed a shift, and was stealing what I told him to steal. In the bar business, that made him employee of the fucking year. So, other than the days we passed each other at 6:30 in the morning, the only time I saw him was on Friday and Saturday nights.

What I saw was somebody who wasn't lazy. He kept up with his side and, when I got too busy, he jumped in if he could. He cleared empties and glasses, threw bottles in front of me when he overheard an order, made change for the machines, and bagged six packs.

He was a quick learner. He didn't wait for me to tell him to restock before the Old Style ran out. And when he saw a customer down to the last few gulps, he asked if he wanted another. He kept the ashtrays and bar clean. But, most of all, he knew something I couldn't teach him. He knew how to read people.

On a Friday night, about one in the morning, Fatboy was busy with a bunch from Zenith.

Dog Breath was one of them. He was a young long-haired guy who wore bib overalls and drove this old powder-blue Ford van with patches of pink Bondo and rust. (He called it "The Love Palace." Inside it was covered with navy-blue shag carpeting. Plus, he'd decked it out with a cooler, a queen-sized mattress and box spring, a brass headrail, a black light, and a poster of a purple Jimi Hendrix. On the back bumper were two stickers: **TO ALL YOU VIRGINS, THANKS FOR NOTHING**, and **DON'T LAUGH, MISTER. YOUR DAUGHTER'S IN HERE.**) And he had this huge gut. He liked to impress us by using it like a shelf and balancing a beer bottle on it.

That night, after he'd gotten a half dozen Old Styles and a few shots in him, he plopped a quarter into the Wurlitzer and played *It's Only Love Doing Its Thing*. And as Barry White pushed out the tune, Dog Breath's friends grabbed pieces of his fat ass and hoisted him up onto the bar. He put his fists into his flabby sides, turned his head, looked up to the ceiling and, in his best Superman voice, hollered, "Behold, motherfuckers! The Dog Breath experience." Then he put his hands behind his head, wiggled his hips, and revolved. We watched waves of flesh roll until the song ended. He was a deranged bastard, but he made me laugh.

Every time Dog Breath came in, he had new story of a woman he'd had in The Love Palace, even though we'd never seen any woman climb in or out of it. But even more than Old Style, whiskey, and imaginary women, he really, really, really loved weed.

Anyway, that night Jerry was selling some grass he'd taken off some kid hanging around Young School. (He'd done it before and, as long as he kept it to just weed and nobody smoked in the bar, I didn't care, provided he slipped me ten bucks, or a dime bag. Either way, it brought in more cash. After Jerry's customers came back from smoking, they bought up bags of chips, which made them thirsty, which made them buy more beer.)

As usual, Jerry took Dog Breath out back first. Jerry didn't smoke dope, so he needed Dog Breath for quality testing purposes. Dog Breath was his loss leader. If he liked it, word would spread, and Jerry could get rid of the rest. If he didn't, he'd have to try to pawn it off on some suckers in Cicero.

When they came back through the door, Dog Breath blew a stream of pot smoke right over the pool table. His eyes were bloodshot and he had this stupid grin on his face.

"Hey," I said. "You gotta respect the establishment."

"Sorry," he said.

When he got to the Wurlitzer, he stopped, put his hands behind his head, dry-humped the machine, and hollered, "It's just love doin' its thing, baby." It was like watching an orca trying to fuck a buoy.

His friends gathered around and started shooting the shit, a buncha loudmouth B.S., like "Betcha that's the only thing he fucks tonight" and "That's because it can't move" and "Hey, that's the only way it happens the rest of the time, too," and all the while Dog Breath kept grinning that stupid grin. I couldn't follow all of it, but here and there I'd catch him pulling one of his buddies aside and cupping his hand to talk in the guy's ear. Then, every fifteen minutes or so, his friends went out back with Jerry, two at a time. They came back smiling too.

Once Jerry dumped all the weed, he had a pocket full of cash. He started shooting pool and made side bets on wild trick shots. He was a terrible gambler and, when he had money, he was reckless. (When he ran out, he'd borrow. He always had a juice loan going and, over the years, I'd lent him money too. I never asked for it back. I knew if I didn't give it to him, he'd borrow more, which just meant less money for Rita and her kids. I knew he thought I was his sucker. Fuck him.) But unlike most nights, he kept making the impossible shots, and he held the table. When the cops, Zeniths, and rest saw that the odds were against them, the line of quarters on the rail dried up.

So Jerry started conning drinkers into games. He knew he had to find something that hit a nerve. If he could, not only would they play, but they'd play angry. If they were pissed, they'd make mistakes. It was a good hustle. So he went for what was sure to make a man lose it. "You always were a pussy," he'd say. "You're a ball-less cocksucker. Go get your sister, faggot."

About the time Jerry had played all the suckers on his side of the bar and was moving his way toward the front, Fatboy told me something was wrong.

"What the fuck do you mean?" I asked.

"Look at Dog Breath. His eyes are glassy. He's about to fall over."

"Yeah. From fuckin' beer and whiskey and dope."

"No. Look at the rest of the group. It's starting to hit them too."

I looked. It was his whole group.

"They're not doin' shit," he said. "They're just standin' there starin' at themselves in the mirror."

They were all holding onto the bar like it was the only thing that could keep them upright. Every once in a while, they'd raise bottles to their lips and take sips of their beer. They were pale and their foreheads were sweaty.

"I asked if they wanted another round," Fatboy continued. "They looked at me like I was shouting from the end of a tunnel."

Just then, Jerry asked Dog Breath if he wanted to shoot a game. Dog Breath shook his head. Jerry said he was a fucking pussy and poked his gut with a cue. Dog Breath still shook his head.

"Come on, ya fat fucker," Jerry said. "Afraid ya might lose an ounce? You're a fat motherfucker who's never screwed a woman in his whole miserable goddamn life. Least not a conscious one. Love Palace? Bullshit palace."

Dog Breath didn't take the bait. I waited for him to explode, but he just kept staring straight ahead, and those little drops of sweat kept rolling down his face.

Like everybody else, Jerry knew Dog Breath still lived at home with his mother. And, like everybody else, he knew he didn't like to talk about it. So, of course, that's where Jerry went next.

"Christ," Jerry said, "Can ya even find your dick under all that? Your ma must hold it for ya when ya piss. Is she a big fat fucker too? Who's got bigger tits? Jesus Christ, how'd she push you out? Musta used the jaws of life. Must have one helluva pussy. Is it true all the guys on the block called her Grand Canyon?"

Dog Breath still didn't take the bait. So Jerry said that he didn't want to play a mama's boy anyway. He turned around, walked back to the pool table, and yelled, "Who's next?"

Dog Breath's jaw was tight and his fingers were white from gripping the bar. I told him to take it easy. He let go of the bar and, for a few seconds, I thought he was going to pull me over and grind my face into floor. But then he grabbed the cash he had on the bar and stomped out.

And I thought that was it.

Jerry gave up hustling pool and joined the other cops who were flirting with some St. Anne's nurses. Railroad Bob came out of the men's room with his fly open and his dick swinging. The nurses and cops laughed.

"Mr. Johnson, Bob," I said.

"Shit," he said. He fumbled with the zipper until his dick was safely put back in his pants. Then he bowed and said, "My apologies, ladies. Life is short, but there's always time for manners."

Then the door swung open and Dog Breath came back in. He wedged himself between his friends, but he kept looking down toward Jerry.

Fatboy asked if he wanted a beer, but Dog Breath didn't speak. He just nodded and threw some cash on the bar. He held one hand over his belly and used the other to keep hold of the bar. He started mumbling through clenched teeth, and he was swaying. Fatboy gave him his beer and cleaned up around him. And that's when he saw it.

Fatboy calmly finished wiping down the bar and emptying Dog Breath's ashtray. Then he walked to the register and motioned to me. While he pretended to make change, he said to me: "You see it?"

"What?"

"That fucker went and got a gun."

I looked over and saw the grip of a Colt .45 peeking out from Dog Breath's bib overalls.

"Fuck."

I usually kept a blackjack in my back pocket just for this kind of thing. But I'd been marching up and down the bar all night and was sick of dragging it with me. So, I'd left it at the other end of the bar and had to go get it before something bad happened. For all my streetwise bullshit, I could be such an idiot.

I thought about grabbing one of the .38s instead, but it would have been stupid to pull a pistol. If I had, I'd have taken the risk of Dog Breath pulling the .45. Plus, I had a bar full of cops with guns. Christ, before long, I could've had bullets flying all over the place and, with my luck, I'd be the one who ended up on a slab.

"How do you want to handle it?" Fatboy asked.

I had to come up with something.

I couldn't tell the cops and have them start shooting. I couldn't go for my gun. It had to be the blackjack.

The one thing I could count on was that a crowded bar of drunks never pays attention to the bartender unless they want a drink. There wcrc timcs when I was so sick of them, I'd stand in the middle of the place giving everybody the finger just to see if they'd notice. They never did.

At last I said: "Give me a minute to get behind him. Then buy them a round of shots."

"Shots?"

"Yeah."

"Why?"

"Shut up and do it."

Fatboy grabbed a handful of shot glasses and the bottle of Jack, and I calmly headed down to the other end of the bar. I reached underneath.

"Want shots?" I heard Fatboy saying.

And, of course, when I need it most, the blackjack wasn't there.

"Want shots?" Fatboy was shouting at Dog Breath's crew, screaming down their drug fog tunnel.

But the fucking blackjack wasn't there and the fear came. Maybe that fuck Donald had taken it. Maybe I'd left it someplace else. Maybe it was upstairs on my dresser. Maybe I'd lost it for good.

I looked up. Fatboy was lining up the shotglasses.

Then I bent down and reached a little farther back and felt the leather handle.

When I came around the bar behind Dog Breath's group, Fatboy was already filling up the shots, pouring each right up to the rim. I got behind Dog Breath right as they started picking them up and throwing them back.

Right when Dog Breath's head snapped back, I kicked his knee from behind, like a kid sneaking up on the playground, and in that same moment I brought the blackjack up on the back of his skull.

It happened so fast nobody noticed.

I stepped out of the way as he fell. His legs gave way and his back hit a table. When he landed, he let out a grunt. The floor rumbled under my feet.

I grabbed the .45, slipped it in my waistband and covered it with my shirt. I looked up. They were finally realizing their friend was on the floor.

"One too many, Dog Breath?" I said. I told Fatboy to give me a cold damp bar towel. I put it on Dog Breath's forehead. I patted his cheeks until he began to moan. Then I asked Dog Breath's friends to help me carry him out.

Dog Breath looked like a fat Gulliver. Drool was seeping out of his mouth. His hands and arms were limp at his side and his legs were spread. Each of his friends grabbed a limb. I held the door while they hoisted him up and squeezed his flabby ass out into the cold December night.

Railroad Bob followed behind them and sang, "The party's over. It's time to call it a day." And the Zeniths, cops, nurses, and Skeletons formed a funeral procession that flowed out of the bar, and onto the sidewalk. Pretty soon they were all singing.

I told them to keep it down. "Fuck it. We're the cops," Jerry said. So I starting singing too.

They opened the van door and wrestled with arms and legs and grappled flab and bib overalls until Dog Breath was mostly inside the Love Palace. They banged his head against the brass bedrail getting him onto the mattress. And at last they crammed his legs in and slammed the door.

Railroad Bob raised his arms and hollered, "The hardest victory is over self."

Then somebody said it was too fucking cold, and they all went inside.

I didn't follow, not right away.

Violence never came natural to me, and afterwards, I always felt sick. I needed a minute. I stood alone on the street. It was so quiet I could hear the click of the traffic light changing. I didn't want to go back in, but I did. Dog Breath left cash on the bar. I needed to get to it before anybody else.

That night, a couple of things became very clear. If I had been working alone, I could have gotten shot. And if he learned to pour a proper shot, Fatboy might work out. They put lines on shot glasses for a goddamn reason.

The Sweet Spot

Angel dust, that's what made Dog Breath want to put a hole in Jerry.

Of course, Jerry hadn't known the weed was laced. But when we told him, he just laughed and said some people couldn't handle their drugs.

Still, I could tell it shook him. After that, his dope dealer days were through. It didn't put too much of a dent in his wallet. Just because he wasn't selling drugs, it didn't mean he couldn't shake down drug dealers. He could count on a few bucks from traffic stops and, like always, he collected for the commander's Hundred Dollar Club.

Pickups were made the last Wednesday of every month. Because I owned a tavern, I was one of the lucky members.

I'd learned early on it was better to pay. My mother held back once. They were there when she opened and closed. On our busiest nights, they carded everybody going in and out, even the Skeletons. The assholes followed our customers and pulled them over for anything. A month of that and we'd have been out of business. So ever since, once a month, they sent somebody around and we handed over the envelope. (Sometimes I was glad I only had to pay a hundred.

Owners running a game or hookers paid double, and had to kick up a percentage to the Outfit, too.)

Jerry and his partner were the bagmen. They weren't picked just because they were crooked. After all, the commander had plenty of criminal cops to choose from. But he'd chosen them because they were reliable, didn't skim the take, and didn't talk about the club to anybody who wasn't in it. In return, they got a monthly kickback. And as long as they answered calls, they could do whatever the hell else they pleased.

Fatboy and I were stacking Old Style in the coolers. The Skeletons and Railroad Bob were watching *Let's Make a Deal*. Monty Hall was onscreen in checkered jacket and slicked-down hair, hustling some guy in bib overalls and a straw hat. Farmer had to choose between $500 or whatever was behind a big curtain on the stage. Fatboy and I stopped to watch.

"Go for the fucking curtain, asshole," Old Man Skeleton said.

"Take the cash," Old Lady Skeleton said.

Farmer jumped up and down. He had this big toothy smile and held a picket sign that said: **Pick me. I aint chicken.** He chose the curtain. A skinny model waved her skinny arm and the curtain rose. Behind it were two mutts in dog houses marked **His** and **Hers**. Old Man Skeleton pounded on the bar like *he'd* lost the $500.

Railroad Bob patted him on the back and said: "Gambling is the son of greed and the father of despair."

"Jesus Christ," Old Man Skeleton said. "Why can't you talk like a regular goddamn person?"

Railroad Bob didn't answer. He looked like a second grader shamed by a teacher. He put his head down and took a few steps to the side. In a low voice, almost a whisper, he ordered an Old Style. I gave it to him. He went back to his booth. Fatboy and I went back to stocking.

Just as the news came on, Jerry came through the back door. He waited at the end of the bar. He always made my pickup last. I opened the register, lifted the drawer, and grabbed the envelope. I gave it to him and he walked out. But a few minutes later, he was back. He was jumpy. He waved me over.

"Can't get the trunk open," he said.

"So? Get another squad car."

"I can't," he said. "Bag's in there. I can't turn in the car like this."

"For fuck's sake." I threw on my hat and grabbed a can of oil from the garage and stepped outside into the cold. Jerry's partner was just standing there, shivering and looking at the trunk like if he stared hard enough, it would magically pop open.

"Good afternoon, Reverend," I sneered.

Alvin "The Reverend" Anderson was a tall thin black guy. Like Jerry, he was in his thirties and had a cop mustache, but unlike Jerry, he was a meticulous bastard. Today, as always, his shoes were spit-shined, and his pants were ironed with razor creases. (Also unlike Jerry, he didn't drink too much, and he knew his fucking Bible like a card counter knows the deck. Hence the nickname. He always wore a military-issue bulletproof vest. He said, no matter what, he was going to retire a healthy man.)

"Good afternoon yourself." From the tone it might as well have been *Go fuck yourself*. He looked at the oil, shook his head, and said: "We're gonna catch hell."

I squirted oil into the lock and slipped the key into it, but it still wouldn't move. Jerry pushed me to one side. He jiggled the key. Nothing. He lost his temper and started trying to force the lock.

"You're gonna break it," the Reverend said.

"Fuck it," Jerry said.

"Well take it to maintenance, then!" (I couldn't see why it was my problem. It's bad enough they made you pay, but to have to help them cart it away...)

Jerry stopped and looked at the Reverend. They both smiled and laughed a little.

"They'll rip us off," the Reverend said.

I felt stupid. But then I thought of something. I told Jerry to stop, and ran back into the bar.

Fatboy, before the dope made him careless, was a damn good thief. Hell, the first time he stole a truck, he was only twelve. (The whole neighborhood knew the story. He'd walked past a truck delivering cheese to Van's, the neighborhood supermarket. The driver had locked the doors and taken the keys, but no matter. Fatboy was behind the wheel in no time. He did it so fast, in fact, that he hadn't stopped to think about how hard it is to sell stolen cheese, or how a twelve-year-old driving a delivery truck is pretty easy to spot. So he'd pulled the thing into an alley, thrown open the doors, and grabbed whatever he could. When the cops found the truck, it'd run out of gas, and was almost empty. But everybody in the neighborhood had fridges stuffed with provolone and Swiss.) Anyway, when I asked him if he could open the trunk without damaging it, he smirked and said, "No problem."

We walked back out to the squad. Jerry and the Reverend were leaning up against it, hunched up against the cold, puffing cigarettes and looking nervous.

Fatboy walked up to the trunk. He bent over it and looked closely. He ran his palm down the middle of it until he was a few inches from the lock. Then he made a fist, raised it above his head, and came down hard on the trunk's lid.

The thing popped right open. And like anybody else would've said the world is round, Fatboy said, "Chevy's got sweet spots."

"Sonuvabitch," Jerry said.

"The Lord provides," the Reverend said.

They grabbed the bag and threw it into the backseat.

And now Fatboy knew about the club, too.

We went back into the bar and started piling bottles again. When we were done, I gave him the list of liquor and chips we needed. He took it and trotted down the stairs.

I sat down on a stool, lit a cigarette, and watched the news. There was a story about some guy who got caught robbing a Wisconsin jewelry store while he was still punched in at his city job. Right in the middle of it, Railroad Bob jumped up. He stomped over to Old Man Skeleton, pointed a finger in his face, and said, "Sometimes I'm so smart I don't even know what the fuck I'm sayin'."

The Ceiling Falls

My mother made me into a pretty good musician. She used to play in the bar. When she was younger, she'd played in clubs. So she knew most people couldn't understand the music. She was able to tune out the drunks. She was tougher than me. I never could.

I still had her black Baldwin upright in the front room of my apartment. Most mornings, after work, I sat down and played. She'd taught me to do more than just bang out a tune. She taught me to let it breathe, to not fill every space with sound, to allow for silence. She taught me to play a ballad slow, really slow, funeral parlor slow.

That morning, I did what I was taught to do. I played "Body and Soul," and the lyrics and tune flowed.

> *My heart is sad and lonely,*
> *For you I sigh, for you, dear, only*
> *Why haven't you seen it*
> *I'm all for you, body and soul*

I shifted the pedals just right. The sound soared and mellowed. At the end of the first verse, I let the note trail off before launching into the second.

> *I spend my days in longing,*
> *And wondering why it's me you're wronging*

I tell you I mean it
I'm all for you, body and soul

I didn't end the note, but let it almost trail off until it collided with the next. But during the third verse, my hand cramped up and the tremors set in. It didn't last long, less than a minute. But I knew.

I stretched out and kept playing. I knew there'd be a day when I couldn't play at all.

When it first showed in my dad, he didn't know what it was. He'd been adopted and didn't know much about his medical history. So he didn't see a doctor for weeks. He thought he was just getting older. But then came the rage.

First I should say that my father had never been an angry man. He didn't let a day begin or end without telling us he loved us. That's what I want to remember first.

For the longest time, my mother refused to get a dryer for the laundry. It would be too expensive, she said, and besides she was happy just carrying it downstairs to hang on a clothesline in the basement. Then one week she was struggling with a heavy load, and she fell down the stairs. When she showed him her bruises, my dad wanted her to go to the hospital, but she laughed and said it was nothing. So he put her on the sofa, tucked a quilt around her, and gave her dinner on a tray. Then he snuck outside in his hat and overcoat, got on the North Avenue bus, and went to Sears. When he got there, he asked the salesman for the best dryer they had. It was delivered the next day.

"This is top-of-the-line," she said when it came through the door. "Do we have the money?"

And he just smiled and said: "For you, we always do."

He treated me that way, too. Even when he should have given me a kick in the ass, he didn't. Sometimes, I wish he had. It would have been easier.

When I was fourteen, I was sitting in the back stairwell smoking a cigarette, and I heard my mother coming. I quickly squished out the butt, threw it in a corner, and ran out the back. But I was too quick. The thing landed behind a cardboard box, and I didn't realize it was still smoldering.

My father was in the basement doing the books. He smelled the smoke and ran upstairs. When he got there, the whole box was on fire. He grabbed a bucket and put it out. Then he went looking for me.

He found me a few blocks away playing softball in an alley. I was at bat when I saw him. The ball was thrown. I let it go by. He stood there with his arms folded looking at me. It was the kind of look that pierces your chest and brings on a flood of shame even before you know what you've done. The guys said hello and asked him how he was. He didn't say anything. He turned and started walking toward the tavern. I dropped the bat and followed.

I sat at the kitchen table with both of them. My father questioned me and, after a while, I admitted what I'd done. I expected him to bounce me off the walls, but instead he told me to look at my mother. "What would it be like to never see or talk to her again?" he said.

"How would you live with yourself if you'd burned her to death?"

He went on until I was crying so hard I couldn't catch my breath. Then he put a hand on my shoulder and told me it was going to be okay.

So those are the memories I like from my dad. But it didn't stay that way.

One day, I was playing an Ella record on the Hi-Fi. He was sitting in his chair reading the *Sun Times*. He told me to shut off the music. Like any teenager, I was a smartass. I told him it was unfair, that it was my house too. He jumped up, ripped the record from the turntable, and threw it across the room. Then he backhanded me across the face, hard.

He sat down and went back to reading the sports page like nothing had happened.

I don't know what surprised me more, that he destroyed an Ella Fitzgerald record or that he hit me, but that's when my mother and I knew there was something wrong.

His disease made every day worse. One minute, he'd buy everyone drinks, and the next he'd ban a regular for nothing. Once, my mother and I found him pointing a pistol at a customer's head. The guy was scared shitless. His eyes were wide and he had his hands stretched above him. My dad said that he was there to rob the place, but the only one with a gun was my father. Every time the guy would start to lower his arms, my dad would holler, "Up!"

My mother saved the guy. She put her arms around my dad and talked to him. "It's alright, honey," she said. "It's alright." He slowly lowered his arms around her. She slipped the pistol out of his hand and slid it down the bar and out of reach. My father kept asking her what was wrong with him and she kept telling him it was going to be alright.

I showed the guy out. He was so scared he kept his arms up until he was in the street. We were lucky. We shared a mutual friend. He didn't call the cops.

More and more, my mother and I took over the bar. During those years, she taught me everything she knew about the business. She was the one who showed me how to keep the books and do inventory. She taught me about payoffs and how not to get ripped off by distributors. She made it possible for me to survive.

After a couple of years, my father could barely walk. He wasn't able to control his arms. We had to dress, feed, and shave him. And what it did to his head was godawful. My mother would come home after long shifts of dealing with the drunks and he'd start screaming at her. He accused her of everything from fucking his friends to planning to kill him.

When he'd come out of it, he'd realize what he'd done, and we'd see the terror in his eyes. He knew everything was slipping away. We spent thousands on doctors, but after a while, we knew it was useless. Eventually, he'd be eating through a stomach tube and breathing from a respirator.

One day, after I'd gone bowling with Jerry, I found a sign on the tavern door: **Closed - Boiler Broken**. Jerry and I went to the apartment. At first, when I saw the envelope on the kitchen table, I thought it was just going to be about another trip to some doctor. Then I saw the words *I'm sorry*, and I knew they were gone.

She said my dad was never going to get better, and trying to fight it would just mean more bills to pay. We'd run out of money, have to sell the business, and be left with nothing. And she said she had to go out with him, otherwise I'd end up spending all the money on lawyers for her. *I'd end up in prison anyway and you'd be broke,* she wrote. *What kind of life would that be?* She told me where I could find the bank books and safety deposit box keys. She told me to call the cops.

But I didn't.

I ran out to the garage. Jerry followed. I opened the door. The fumes poured out. I held my breath and threw open the roll top. The cloud of exhaust cleared and I saw them. They were slumped to one side. His head was tilted back and his mouth was open. She sat next to him with her head against his chest and arm around his shoulder. Their faces were cherry red, like they'd fallen asleep on the beach.

I tried to open the driver's door, but she'd locked it. Jerry grabbed a tire iron and smashed the window. He pulled open the door and turned off the engine. He dragged her out and laid her on the cement in the alley. Then he did the same for my father.

I pumped on my mother's chest while Jerry gave her mouth-to-mouth. A neighbor must've called because, after about fifteen minutes, the paramedics showed up. But by then I knew it was useless. She was gone.

I used to wonder why we didn't try to help my dad, but now I know that it was because my mother was right. I'd loved him, but he wasn't my father anymore. He was this thing that'd become a weight on me.

Huntington's is a family disease. I was told I had a 50/50 chance of getting it. It usually hits in your thirties. So, when my hand cramped up, the fear hit me, and when it happened again, I could only think of one person to tell.

I went to see her when her kids were in school and Jerry was at work. When she opened the door, she was wearing a sweatshirt with little splotches of paint on it, and her hair was covered with a scarf. Her face lit up. She smiled that smile with the little gap. She raised her eyebrows, grabbed my shirt with one hand and pulled me inside.

"I want you to see something," she said. I followed her down into the basement. She'd converted the coal shed into a work space. She said the light was terrible, but it had a lock to keep her kids out.

She had canvases, brushes, paints, palettes, and an easel crammed under the single bulb, and there were crates of finished paintings. She kept snapshots on a pegboard of neighborhood buildings: taverns, bowling alleys, bungalows and two-flats.

She showed me the painting she was working on. Two kids played softball in an alley under a street light. One player watched the ball with the bat at his side. The other waited with outstretched hands. On a garbage can there was a quart of beer and a pack of cigarettes.

Next to it, a man dressed in a white t-shirt and gray work pants smoked a cigarette and watched.

I told her it was great. It was.

She made coffee and we sat at the kitchen table. Even though I'd taken her away from her painting, she said she was glad to see me. It took me a few minutes, but I finally blurted it out. "I've got it," I said.

Her face dropped and she looked like the ceiling had fallen down on her. She asked if I was sure. I told her about the piano, and how it'd happened again the next day.

"I think I'm starting to lose my balance a little when I walk," I said. "Nobody will notice, unless they know."

I said that, for now, I could explain I was just getting clumsy, but in a year, maybe two, excuses wouldn't work anymore.

She reached across the table and took my hand. She pulled me closer and kissed me. She told me she'd see me whenever she could. "Just us," she said.

I'd broken it off with her about a month after we were sure about my dad.

We were still in high school. I brought her down into the basement of the tavern and, there, with the sound of drunks above us, I told her that there was a good chance I'd get it. I told her that I loved her and would always love her, but I could never marry her or any other woman. Her face dropped and the tears came.

She told me that it didn't matter, and that she'd take the chance. The chance? Christ. She was sixteen. What the fuck did she know? What the fuck did any of us know?

Man Pleads Guilty to Killing Boss

by James Thompson

PAUL GARDNER, 38, pled guilty today to the murder of his former supervisor, William Connor, 54.

Mr. Gardner, a former Zenith employee, was laid off in October, 1978. Shortly after losing his job, he confronted Mr. Connor in the Zenith employee parking lot and accused his former supervisor of being the reason for his firing.

After a brief discussion, Mr. Connor got into his car and left. Gardner then followed him to the Sears store on Harlem and North and again insisted on speaking with him.

Due to the cold weather, Mr. Connor got into Gardner's van. When Gardner again accused his former boss of singling him out and giving him a negative reference, Mr. Connor laughed. Police say Gardner then became enraged, drew a .22 pistol, and shot Mr. Connor in the head, chest, and abdomen. He then placed Mr. Connor's body in the back of the van and drove home.

When Sears' management reported the victim's abandoned car and his wife reported him missing, police began an investigation.

A break occurred when Gardner attempted to cash Mr. Connor's paycheck at a currency exchange. A suspicious clerk called police and delayed Gardner until they arrived. A search warrant was then obtained for Gardner's home. Mr. Connor's decomposing body was found in the basement under several bags of cement.

Zenith management said that Mr. Gardner's dismissal had nothing to do with his job performance or any negative evaluation from Mr. Connor. "It was simply a matter of economics," said Zenith spokesman Alfred Simmons.

Gardner's sentencing hearing is set for this Monday.

Everybody's Got a Zenith

Once the tremors started, I knew I didn't have a lot to look forward to.

I knew I'd end up in a bed somewhere pissing and shitting on myself. And I didn't want it to be some state-run shithole where everyone watched TV like zombies and waited to die. I wanted it to be a bed with clean sheets, and people who were paid enough to really take care of me. But that meant I'd need money. Real money.

I'd saved some, and I could sell the building and license once it came to that, but it was hard to say what good that would do me. And even if I'd gotten the price I could've gotten five years earlier, it would never be enough. It'd take a few years for me to die. I needed another way.

People with money hide the fact they're ripoff artists. They like to pretend that they got rich because they were smarter or worked harder. For some reason, they've got to lie to themselves.

Nobody I knew believed in that work-hard-get-ahead bullshit. On any given day, we bought and sold stolen aluminum siding, storm windows, cigarettes, booze, car parts, tools, golf clubs, TVs, stereos, VCRs, and anything else you could think of.

I grew up knowing how much inspectors were bribed. I knew to keep a ten wrapped around my license just in case I was pulled over. I knew that precinct captains registered dead people to vote and that priests sure as hell skimmed Sunday's collection.

By the time I was in high school, I never left the apartment without a twenty in my pocket. It was life insurance. My mother called it robbery money. If you got robbed and the thief didn't like the take, he just might shoot you for the crime of not having enough.

So I knew what made the world go 'round. And I knew I needed more.

I thought about running numbers, a game, or juice loans. But building up that kind of business would take time I didn't have. Then it came to me. I had a customer base. Why not offer them merchandise they could purchase at half price? Why not launder the profits through the bar? Why not get that merchandise as cheap as I could? When it came to free procurement, I was no expert, but I had an employee with years of experience. And, the best part, I knew two cops who never passed up a good scam. I just had to convince all of them it was worth the risk.

It was early on a Friday night. Stocking was finished and we were leaning against the back bar waiting for the rush. Railroad Bob had been in the men's room for twenty minutes, and the Skeletons were hunched over full beers. I asked Fatboy how things were going with Zenith.

"Nothin' yet," he said.

"Really?" I said.

"Just a matter of time."

"You sure?"

"Yeah." But he looked away when he said it and didn't sound sure.

"You know, sales have been dropping here for at least a year. At first, I thought I was being ripped off, but...it's the Zeniths. Nobody's buyin' 'em. I give 'em two years and they'll close."

He smirked, laughed a little, and said, "Bullshit. They won't close. Everybody's got a Zenith."

"Everybody *had* a Zenith," I said. "Japs are killin' 'em. Stores can't move 'em. But I've got a business idea. A way to make up the difference. We could set up a little store of our own."

"A store?" he smirked.

"Kind of."

"What, you're gonna start up something new in this neighborhood?"

"We'll just run it out of the garage."

"You're joking." He laughed and shook his head. "You're serious."

"It doesn't have to be forever," I went on. "In a year you'll have enough to get out. Get into a trade. Start a business. In the meantime, you can be the...head of procurement."

He said nothing, but his eyes just sort of narrowed and he looked at me funny.

"Even if you do get caught, we'll have enough to take care of it," I went on. "And, if the worst thing happens and you do time, you'll have the money when you get out."

He folded his arms, shifted his feet, and looked at me like I was crazy. At last he spoke. "It's easy for people to talk about doing time when they never have."

We were cut short. Railroad Bob came out of the men's room hiking up his pants and struggling with his belt. "Sombody's rippin' off TP," he said.

I looked over at Old Lady Skeleton. She was lugging around this big old dirty purse.

"Hand it over," I said.

"What?" she asked.

"Hand it over or get lost."

"Give him the fucking thing," Old Man Skeleton said.

She gave me the bag. I reached into it and pulled out three rolls of toilet paper.

"Gotta stop," I said.

"Sorry," she said.

Railroad Bob put his arm around her shoulder and said "Little thieves get caught. Big thieves get rich."

"Cheese eater," Old Lady Skeleton said. Then she pouted and looked at me, and said, "We're all out. We've been wipin' with the *Sun Times* for a week."

I threw one of the rolls back into the goddamn bag and gave it back to her. To Fatboy I said: "Everybody's a thief. Only difference is how they justify it."

We stood in front of a long row of glowing TV screens. Each had the volume turned down and was set to a different channel. There was everything from portables to consoles. There were Sonys, Panasonics, and Silvertones, the Sears brand. Finally, at the end, a few Zeniths had been shoved into a corner and marked for clearance.

The salesman's name tag said *Ron*. He looked exactly like what you'd expect a goddamn appliance salesman to look like. He had a crew cut, checkered pants, and a short-sleeved shirt with a bunch of pens in his pocket. He had this toothy smile, the kind companies always paint onto employees to go along with the bullshit sales pitch they had drilled into them.

Fatboy asked why the Zeniths were on clearance. Ron babbled on about quality and variety, but then, when he figured we weren't going to buy anything, he gave up trying sell us. "Nobody beats the Japs on price," he said and walked away.

Then Fatboy asked me how the Japs were able to do it. "Don't they gotta pay to bring stuff in?" he asked. "Don't they gotta pay their people?"

"Does it matter? It's the way it is," I said. "Zenith's done."

We walked down the line of TVs. Fatboy had ditched his ratty jean jacket for a big army surplus overcoat. When we got to the smallest Silvertone portables, he stopped and looked around for Ron. He grabbed one of the portables and we started walking. When we got near the escalator, he put the portable under his coat.

I'd stolen from the government. There was always the thought I might get caught. But it was a fear that always felt down the road. This was different. As we rode the escalator up to the main floor and walked out, the fear was close and real. There wasn't a second I didn't expect to feel a hand grab my arm.

As we crossed the parking lot and sat down on the bus stop bench, the fear faded and there was relief.

But there was more. Thieves always talk about the rush of ripping somebody off, and they're right. I felt that. But there was something else. I'd never felt it stiffing the government or shortchanging drunks. That was just business. But this was different.

I felt like we'd done something right.

◇◇◇

Fatboy's apartment was nothing. A combination bedroom/living room, a kitchen area, a bathroom, and a closet. He'd made a table of wood and cinderblocks.

On top of it there was an old portable radio and a lamp. There was a mattress covered in blankets on the floor. No box springs, even.

We sat on stools in the kitchen. He took the Silvertone from its box. Then he took a screwdriver and removed the screws that attached the chassis to the case. When he took the case off there was a small metal plate. He threw the screwdriver on the table, sat back, and said: "Lyin' bastards."

I took a look. Engraved on the plate was *Toshiba*.

"Ya know," he said. "When I was kid, even when it was really hot, I never wore shorts. Rita neither. You ever been hit with a cat-o-nine tails?"

"No," I said.

"The fucker never woke us up. We'd be in a deep sleep. The kind you only know as a kid. The leather would cut into us. We'd scream and jump from one side of our beds to the other. We'd try to time it. Sometimes ya got it. Sometimes ya didn't. We used to scream for him to stop. We'd beg him. He never would. We'd jump from our beds and run through the house. That would piss him off even more, 'cause he couldn't keep up. But, once in a while, he'd still get us with one. Finally, he'd get too tired and sit in his chair with that fucking whip still in his hand." Fatboy leaned forward in his chair. "But it stopped when I was sixteen. He kept it in his top dresser drawer. I heard them whispering after he came home. I heard Rita's name. She'd done something that day, and Ma never forgot when somebody broke one of her rules." Fatboy's eyes bored into me. "When I heard that drawer slide open, I jumped outta bed and ran to her room before he could start. I put him into a choke hold." Fatboy swallowed hard. "He's smaller than me, but strong. He pushed back and slammed me against the wall. I had to bang his head a few times before he let it go. I shoved him from the room and slammed him into the dining room table. I whipped that bastard until Rita begged me to stop. I told him if he ever hit us again, I'd kill him. My mother just stood there with her mouth open. After years of him beating us, she looked at me like I was the monster. I went back to my room. He never touched us again."

I said nothing.

Fatboy put the TV back together. "Lyin' sack of shit," he said. "There was never any goddamn job. Fuck it. I'm in."

Once a month, Jerry and I played poker in the basement of Duff's Bar, a Cicero tavern on 16th Street. It was open 23 hours a day. During the one hour it was closed, the owner, Brain, locked the door, threw out the ones who had no money, swept up around the ones who did, and opened up again. There were people who cashed their paychecks in that place and didn't come out for days.

It was an old bar, but Brain, like everybody else who bought into that faggot disco shit, was trying to cash in. Everything, the bar, the stools, and the floor, was white tile, pleather, or Formica. There was a mirrored ceiling and one of those twirling disco balls. It did wonders for my mood. There's nothing like seeing a piss-stained street drunk throwing up on the bar while the jukebox spits out *I love the night life, I love to boogie* over and over again until you're praying to whatever God there is to please, if there is any mercy, rip your ears from your fucking head.

At the end of the bar was the DJ booth. It was filled with old speakers, stacks of records, and cases of beer. Next to it was the basement door. To get through that door you had to know a cop, or be one.

Brain was tall and skinny. He wore black-rimmed glasses with lenses so thick I could never tell what the hell he was looking at. He kept his fingernails long. He said it made picking up chips and cards easier. He was a good dealer and a better bookie. He had a gift for odds and points. He did a side business in juice loans backed by the Outfit.

We sat around a worn green felt-covered octagon table, drinking beer and throwing chips into pots that rose and shrunk. I bided my time, waiting for the right moment to bring up my little business opportunity. Meanwhile, as always, Jerry held court with a story. This time it was about a drunk doctor who'd rear ended his squad.

"This fuckin' guy. I could see walking up to his car, even. Gold watch, gold wedding band, gold cufflinks, fuckin' gold tie tack. Everything fuckin' gold," Jerry said. "He's got finger nails like a fag and his hair styled."

Brain and I were glued to the story. The Reverend was stacking his poker chips in neat little stacks, all neat and meticulous, but even he cocked his head sideways.

"So this fuckin' guy, he's tryin' like hell to keep his head straight, but he looks like one of those fuckin' bobble dogs the 'Ricans got in the back of their rides. So I get up there, and I see the doctor's bag lyin' on the front seat, and when he rolls down the window there's this...blast of smell. Like I'm glad he wasn't smoking, because the booze in the fumes...I mean, he just reeked of scotch, so I'm thinkin' ca-fucking-ching."

The Reverend had arranged all the chip stacks, and now he was evening them out. Jerry gave him a little look, like: why wasn't he paying full attention?

"So I ask him if he's been drinkin', and he says he had two at Toppers," Jerry went on. "So, I say, 'If I look in that bag, am I gonna find a bottle?' And I got the fucker, 'cause he puts his head back and stares at the ceiling and says, 'Jesus.' And I says to him, 'Jesus ain't gonna help ya, Doc.' So, what does the stupid motherfucker do? Reaches in his pocket, pulls out his wallet, and starts flashin' cash for all the world to see."

The Reverend smirked a little. Jerry didn't seem to like that.

"I got civilians watching me," he went on. "I gotta make it look good. I says real loud, 'No, sir. You can't pay for the ticket now. You'll have to do it by mail.' Then I lean in and tell him to put a twenty around the license, and pass it to me. I pretend to write the ticket while the Reverend helps him get into a parking spot without killin' anybody."

I looked over at the Reverend. He'd re-leveled most of the stacks of chips, but one was shorter than the rest, so he started redistributing it among the others. Jerry noticed my attention had wandered, and this time he gave me a look. But he pressed on.

"So the Reverend tells him to get out and leave the keys. He looks confused, but he does what he's told. He asks me if we got a deal. Jesus Christ, he's so fuckin' stupid. It's 5:30, there's tons a people walkin' home and waitin' for busses, and this idiot is askin' if we got a deal. So I got pissed. I tell him to shut up and get on the sidewalk. The asshole can barely make it. He's gotta grab onto a meter. I roll up the windows, put the keys in the visor, lock it up, and slam the door. And I tell him to start walkin'. And what does the whiney little cocksucker do? He says, 'I thought we had a deal?' Like he gets off for twenty and he thinks he's gonna drive his drunk ass through *my* neighborhood? So while the Reverend stands guard, I drag Dr. Kildrunky into a hallway. I slam him against the wall, stick my club in his face, and say, 'One more word and I will fuck you with this.'"

The Reverend was still doing his master builder bit with the chips, but he gave a little nod, like: Yeah, he said it.

"Man, his face goes white. And he starts bawlin'. What is it with these Joe College assholes? You give 'em a little shove and they start wailin' like little girls. So, I figure he's got the message and me and the Reverend leave."

The Reverend's chip stacks were finally perfect, like he'd aligned them with a fuckin' laser. He leaned back and nodded like he'd just built the fuckin' Sears Tower. Jerry gave him another dirty look, but kept going.

"So about twenty minutes later, we're drivin' back down North Avenue and this rookie, fuckin' brand new cop, is standin' by the car shovin' a slim jim in the window! And Dr. Drunkie's leanin' against the car watchin' him. We pull up. I get out. When Drunkie sees me, his eyes bug and he walks away fast. I ask the rookie what he's doin'."

"'Guy locked his keys in the car,' he says. 'Helpin' him.'"

"'I did it. He's drunk, I says."

"And what does this motherfuckin' rookie cop say? 'Well he gave me twenty. You can have half.'"

By then, we were all leaning in a little. Even the Reverend, even though he'd been there.

"What'd ya do?" Brain asked.

"I took the whole fuckin' twenty!" Jerry beamed proudly, like he was fuckin' Cop of the Year. "Fuckin' rookie. Me and the Reverend went to White Castle's."

"Rookies gotta learn," the Reverend said.

"Everybody's gotta learn," Jerry said.

"You got that right."

And Jerry leaned back and kicked under the table, just hard enough to bobble it so all the neat stacks of chips toppled over. He grinned like the fuckin' cat that devoured a whole pet store full of canaries.

"Motherfucker!" It was the first swearing I'd heard from the Reverend in a while.

Brain and I just shook our heads. Cops being assholes. Nothing new.

On the other hand, I knew the Reverend would have his revenge. And that fit my purposes just fine.

As the night wore on, my stack and Brain's both went down a little. But damn near all Jerry's chips started going across the table. And after a while, Jerry had to hit up Brain for a loan, and those chips started heading across the table, too. Pot after pot after pot. And the Reverend would line 'em up again, and stack 'em up again, higher and higher, and Jerry would kick the table again, but as the night wore on it felt different. Not pride and assholeishness, but anger and frustration. The last time he did it, the Reverend didn't even complain.

"What, you're fuckin' mute now?" Jerry said.

"I think the size of the stacks says enough," the Reverend said. Which was funny because Jerry no longer had one.

After that, Jerry and I sat at the bar drinking beer. At the beginning of the game, you couldn't shut him up, but now he was quiet. For all his big talk about shoving people around and being the man of his house, he knew he'd have to go home and face Rita with empty pockets and bills to pay. He sat there hunched over, staring at his beer bottle, slowly peeling off the label. I waited for reality to sink deep.

"Want to go in on somethin'?" I said at last.

"What?" he said.

"Me and Fatboy got somethin'," I said.

"Ain't goin' in with no junkie," he said.

I didn't say anything. There was no rush. I needed to let this little tidbit mix in with all his money troubles and the beer, so all of it could settle into his gut. The desperate never need much of a pitch. I bought a couple more rounds until finally he looked up from his beer and said, "What ya got?"

As I told him the scheme, I watched the desperation fade and a smile spread across his face. I knew he'd go for it. Not just for the money, but for the risk. With every word I spit, I could see the adrenaline rushing through him. He sat with head raised, back straight. When I knew he was hooked, I asked him if the Reverend would go along. He laughed. "There's money," he said. "He's in."

And that was all it took.

Ain't Scared

I went to see Rita whenever I could.

I'd walk down her alley and, when I was sure no eyes were on me, I'd make my way through the little yard to her back door. Usually, I didn't have to knock. She'd swing the door open, pull me inside, and kiss me.

Sometimes we had sex, but a lot of times, and the ones I remember most, we'd sit in her kitchen talking, smoking cigarettes and drinking coffee. Sitting there listening and watching her was how I always pictured it would have been if we'd married.

She wasn't much of a housekeeper. There were usually dishes in the sink and dirty pans on the stove. The floor seemed to always need mopping. But I didn't care, because she was sitting there with me. I was able to listen to the music of her voice and watch the sweep of her hand as she lifted a cigarette to her mouth or brushed her hair back. Those hours were a gift she gave me. There were plenty of men she could have given them to, but she chose me and I was grateful for it.

One day, she was laying across my lap on the couch. Between puffs of her cigarette, she talked about art. "It's the one thing that's mine," she said.

"I'm yours," I pointed out.

She smiled a little. "I'm serious. I don't think about my kids. Jerry. Any of it."

"Yeah. It's nice when everything disappears."

Her face lit up. She smiled and kissed me.

I told her that when I played music, everything else faded. When it was the best, I was soaked in it. There was no time. There was no neighborhood. There was no world. Best of all, there was no me.

But for her it was different. Her painting didn't get her out of the world, but deeper in it. "There's a lot that's shitty about this place," she said. "The crime. The frustration. But there are things that are beautiful about it too. I love, at dusk, when the street lights click on and they mix with the sunlight. There's this amber blanket over everything. I love the boys taking drags on their cigarettes while waiting for their turn at bat. I love the girls huddled together to keep warm while they wait for a bus. I love a perfect row of parking meters. Christ, I even like after garbage pickup when the lids are left scattered over the alleys. When I paint, I have to set a timer. If I don't, I get too lost in it."

Sitting there listening to her, it was me who got lost. Even during the worst of it, even when we fought, even years before when I had to break it off with her, any moment with her made me feel the same way the music did. In that kitchen, I could see and hear nothing but her. If I could've, I would have stayed there forever.

◇◇◇

It was late on a Tuesday night. We sat across from the parking lot in the squad. Fatboy and I sat in the back. Jerry and the Reverend sat up front.

We'd spent days looking at Sears. What we saw made it a good score. It wasn't far from the tavern, but was outside of the neighborhood. It was an L-shaped cinderblock box with display windows. The North Avenue side of it blocked any view of the parking lot, main entrance, and loading dock. The delivery trucks were parked in front of the dock. All of it gave us cover, and we could use the hand trucks to haul away the shit. All we needed to get past the locks was a hammer and screwdriver. Fatboy loved the alarm system. It was old and cheap.

Jerry was fidgety. He kept puffing on a cigarette and gripping the steering wheel. The Reverend was calmly reading the paper by the dome light.

"Let's go," Jerry said.

"Somebody's in there," Fatboy replied.

"Bullshit. Nobody works this late."

Fatboy pointed to a car in the parking lot, and to slivers of light shining through the blinds on the third floor of the building. "That's an office."

"Somebody forgot to turn out the light," Jerry said. "And some asshole broke down in the lot."

The car was a spotless new red Corvette that glowed under the lot lights. It was parked on a slant so nobody could park too close.

The Reverend put down his paper, and said, "Would you leave a car like that in a fucking parking lot overnight?"

"This is bullshit," Jerry said.

"Puss head."

"Bible fucker." Jerry stared at that car like he was gunning for it.

Finally the third-floor light switched off. Ten minutes after that, a man came out of the back door, locked up, and walked toward the Corvette. When he got to the car, he threw the briefcase onto the passenger's seat. He took off his overcoat. Underneath, he wore a green checkered leisure suit, white tie, and yellow shirt. Christ, he looked radioactive.

"Holy shit," Jerry said. "It's fucking Bob Barker."

"We're comin' on down, Bob," the Reverend said. And we laughed as we watched Leisure Suit pull out of the parking lot. And Jerry said that we should do it, but Fatboy told him to wait fifteen minutes.

"Jesus Christ, why?" Jerry said.

"Could've forgot somethin'," the Reverend told him.

"You're a natural," Fatboy observed.

It was true. The Reverend liked a joke, but wasn't a clown. He liked to gamble, but wasn't a sucker. He was as crooked as any of the others, but he didn't piss away his money. According to Jerry, he lived far away from family and old friends. He had a condo on the lake, a one-bedroom in a high rise with a doorman. He was smart.

Jerry got sick of waiting and decided to kill time by being an asshole. He looked at Fatboy through the rearview mirror and said: "So. Mr. Krause."

Since Fatboy'd been out, I don't think anybody'd so much as mentioned Mr. Krause to him. I almost had, but I'd figured it was none of my business and I had my own shit to worry about.

A wave of anger came over Fatboy. "What?"

"Did you do it?" Jerry always expected everybody to forget about his debts, but he never let anybody else off the hook.

"No," Fatboy said.

Mr. Krause lived across the street from Fatboy and Rita's father. He was an old guy and lived alone. One Wednesday afternoon, neighbors complained of a thick stench coming from the house. The cops came around to find a window smashed, a door unlocked, and the old man face down on the floor.

At first, they thought he'd had a heart attack, but their police skills kicked in when they saw the bloodstain on the carpet, and the brains spilling out of the black gash on the side of his skull. His wedding ring and watch were gone. The place had been ripped apart. The examiner said he'd been killed the day before.

The day the cops found the old man's body, Jerry asked me to take a ride. We found Fatboy in a dope house on Massasoit. He was nodding off on a cot. There were junkies shooting up all over the damn place.

At first, the dealer gave us a hard time about dragging him out. Fatboy still had money left, and we were cutting into his profits. Jerry flashed his badge and told him to fuck off.

We got Fatboy to his feet and dragged him out to the alley. Jerry had an old van he used for camping. We pushed him into the back and told him to lie on the floor and keep his mouth shut. Jerry told Fatboy that, no matter what happened, if he wanted to stay out of prison, to do what he was told.

When we got into the garage, Jerry told him to get up, but he was still blasted. So we yanked him by his arms until he was sitting up. Jerry slapped him hard in face.

"What the fuck are you doing?" Fatboy asked.

"Saving your sorry ass," Jerry said.

We got him on his feet. I held him up while Jerry made sure it was clear. Then we dragged him through the yard to the back door.

When we got him inside, Rita told us to take him straight to the bathroom. We held him up while she stripped him. Then we threw him into a cold shower.

"What the fuck are you doing?" Fatboy was pissed. We were making him come down, a waste of good dope.

"Shut the fuck up, you junkie fuck," Rita said. "You're in a lotta trouble."

"I'm always in trouble," he said.

After twenty minutes in the shower, fifteen minutes of us walking him around, and a few more slaps, he was straight enough to understand.

Rita told him about Mr. Krause, and that the cops were looking for him. He said that it was bullshit, that he hadn't been anywhere near the place, and that, for the last few days, he'd been in the dope house.

"Shootin' dope, even if it's true, is one shitty alibi, asshole," Rita said. "Think they'll believe you? Think they won't put your ass in jail?"

Line by line, Rita fed him the story. He was with her all that day. In the morning, they'd gone downtown to shop at Marshall Field's. After, they'd stopped at the Berghoff and had a beer and sandwich. Then they walked over to the Art Institute to look at the Joan Miro sculptures. After that, they took the El home. She was smart. She picked times and places that would have been packed with people. Nobody could say they weren't there.

She made him tell the story over and over. Jerry played detective, asking him questions, trying to trip him up. But, in the end, it sounded real, and even I began to think it was true.

When the cops came around, even though they still thought Fatboy had murdered the old man, the alibi was good and there was no hard evidence. And because Jerry was his brother-in-law, they couldn't beat a confession out of him. So he was never charged.

Now Jerry was being an asshole asking about it. But I understood. I never pictured Fatboy as a killer, but you never know what a junkie will do. I always wondered about it myself.

Jerry pulled the squad into a space between the trucks. He and the Reverend got out and stood lookout. When Jerry lit another cigarette, the Reverend snatched it from his mouth and squashed it.

Fatboy and I grabbed the tools. Fatboy shoved a Slim Jim into the window frame of one of the trucks and opened the cab. He climbed in, jammed a screwdriver into the ignition lock, gave it a crank, and started the truck. I laughed a little. He was so quick. Seconds.

We popped open the truck's roll top door. Then we grabbed a dumpster and pulled and pushed until it was under the alarm box. Fatboy climbed up onto the dumpster. I handed him cans of liquid Styrofoam. He sprayed the shit into the alarm box until the foam oozed out of it. As they emptied, he dropped the cans. They bounced and clanked onto the cement. The noise made me jump.

We waited in the truck. My hands were shaking and I was breathing quickly. The steam fogged the windows.

"It's normal," Fatboy said.

"What?" I said.

"Fear."

"Ain't scared."

"Uh-huh."

When he was sure the Styrofoam had set, Fatboy grabbed a hammer and screwdriver. Then, like he was working an assembly line, he moved from one door to the next and popped locks. Bang...bang...bang.

Then we waited. The squad's radio squawked and hissed. We heard a truck rumbling down North Avenue. Its brakes whined as it came closer. It stopped and idled. And I knew it couldn't be a Sears truck and that it'd just stopped for the North and Harlem light, but that didn't stop me from flinching. Fatboy put a hand on my shoulder. Then we heard the sounds of gears grinding and the truck lurching forward.

When we were certain nobody'd called in, Jerry jumped up on the platform. We threw the doors open and grabbed flatbed carts. Fatboy led the way with a flashlight.

I remember the rumbling of the carts, and the jumping of the beam.

I remember Jerry behind me bumping his cart against the back of my legs and laughing.

I remember hearing myself mumble, but not knowing what I said.

Then, over and over, I remember whispering to myself to shut up. But I couldn't.

We rolled straight for the TVs and VCRs. We worked like a bucket brigade, passing boxes from one to the other. I screwed up the cadence once and missed. The box flew past me and smashed into a pyramid display of radios. Jerry laughed as the things crashed down and slid across the floor.

When our merchandise was piled high, we pushed the carts back. Jerry played bumper cars with his. He banged display cases and mannequins. A few boxes fell off his cart.

"Stop fuckin' around," I said.

"Why?" He said. "It's fun."

Through it all, he never looked scared, and I could never figure out why. If I'd been him, I wouldn't have even been there. I'd have been the straightest cop the world had ever seen, a fucking Boy Scout. Every day, I'd have done anything to make sure I went home to her.

But he did everything he could to stay away. If he wasn't at my place, he was playing cards. If he wasn't playing cards, he was at the track. If he wasn't doing that, he was fucking some stripper he kept on the side. And now this.

We went back and forth loading and unloading the carts until the truck was just about full. We left only the display models and the Zeniths.

Jerry and the Reverend took off first in the squad. Fatboy grabbed a few hand trucks from the dock and threw them in the truck. Then he closed the loading dock doors and we got the fuck out of there, too.

It was cold, but the sweat had soaked my shirt. Even when we were blocks from Sears, my hands still shook. My eyes kept shifting from the street to the side mirrors. Fatboy told me to relax and that it was going to be okay.

"You're so goddamn calm," I said.

"Scared shitless," he said. "Always."

He looked over and smiled, and it helped. I felt my stomach loosen a bit. He was careful. He took side streets and drove a few miles under the speed limit. When he came to stop signs, it was straight out of *Rules of the Road*.

We pulled into the alley next to the bar. The truck's lights lit up the squad. Jerry was leaning on a fender smoking a cigarette and drinking a beer. The Reverend was sitting in the driver's seat with his head resting against the window. He put his hand up to block the light. He looked at us like we were moochers ringing his door bell.

When Jerry saw us, he put down his beer on the hood of the squad and started clapping. He kept it up even after we'd parked and gotten out.

"Jesus Christ, stop already," I hissed. "The neighbors are gonna hear."

The motherfucker honestly looked sad that he had to stop. "You worry too much."

"Somebody's got to."

"What's it get ya?"

"Not jail."

I opened the garage door. Fatboy jumped up into the truck and handed down the hand trucks. Jerry loaded and I stacked until the boxes covered the wall, floor to ceiling. I put three ten-gallon gas cans and some newspapers in the truck and locked up the garage.

◇◇◇

Under the Central Street Bridge there was a large dirt patch, a deserted spot separated from the rail yard by a tall chain-link fence. The only way in or out was an access road. The Reverend parked the squad at the mouth of it to stand watch.

Jerry, Fatboy, and I soaked the truck with gas, splashing the stuff everywhere, staining our pants and shoes. The fumes burned my nostrils and made my throat raw. We rolled up thick wads of newspaper and lit them. The yellow flames made our faces glow. We threw the torches in. A blue wave spread over the inside of the truck. Soon, clouds of black smoke poured out, and flames rose until the whole underside of the bridge was lit up orange.

We trotted back to the squad and got in. As the Reverend pulled away, he rolled down his window. Jerry said it was too cold, but the Reverend said he was tired and the stink of the gas was making him dizzy. "I'll wrap this fucker around a pole," he said.

As we drove back, I got this heavy feeling, like I'd been pounding spikes all night. I couldn't keep my eyes open. I fought sleep. It was a fight I couldn't win. But right before I gave in, I heard Jerry laugh. "Jesus Christ," he said. "Jesus fucking Christ."

◇◇◇

Word spread quickly.

Within a week, I'd sold TVs and VCRs to half the cops in the district. And even though they were always talking about the Japanese stealing their jobs, the Zeniths couldn't pass up on Sonys and Toshibas. I was sure I'd have the rest sold by the end of the month. But even where I lived, there were cops who played it straight. And on a cold Wednesday in mid-December, one of them paid me a visit.

Frank Olsen was a lieutenant, a by-the-booker who was always hassling somebody about some bullshit. Behind his back, the other cops called him Adolf and, when he'd pass, they'd click their heels. I'd only seen him once before. When he first transferred into the district, he stopped in to try and catch guys drinking on duty. He did, but the commander told him to lay off and he never came back. Until now.

Except for Railroad Bob, the place was empty. But bad old Adolf Olsen just stood there waiting to be noticed, looking like he'd walked out of a cop show. His coat was pressed, and his badge was a mirror. His shirt was bleached white and starched. He had his cap tucked under his arm. His head was a cinder block covered with a field of gray cut close to the scalp. He just stood there, right inside the door. And as he surveyed the room, he gave the place a look like it'd give him a disease.

Railroad Bob looked up from his booth. "There's no situation a cop won't make worse," he said.

"Shut up, Bob."

Adolf said he needed to speak with me in private. I said we could talk in the back. A payoff was a longshot, but I grabbed a hundred from the till.

We stood in the back stairway. One door led to the alley and the other to the garage. He stood between them and gave me a look.

"I hear you're in the VCR business," he said.

"Somebody's tellin' stories," I told him.

"Really?"

"Yes, sir."

He pointed at the door to the garage and said, "What if I open it?"

The fucker had me. I could holler about a warrant, but we were alone. He'd just trump up some probable cause bullshit and bust me anyway.

Even when you're pretty sure a cop can be bribed, you have to be careful. They don't like to be reminded they're criminals. And the others don't like to think about the criminals they work with. If you ask, and the cop gets pissed off, he'll tack on charges. In a second, you can go from a guy who ran red lights to a cop beater. Before you know it, you'll be buried so far inside Cook County that, even with the best lawyer, it'll be days before you see the street.

I wasn't sure at all. But I had to chance it. "Is there any way we can work this out, sir?" I made a show of reaching for my wallet.

But he just walked right past me and opened the garage door. He switched on the light and looked over all the TVs and VCRs. He knew. And he knew that I knew that he knew.

He grabbed a VCR and walked back.

"Wife's been beggin' for a nice Christmas present," he said. "I was never here."

"Right."

He nodded toward the backdoor. I opened it. He walked out and put the box in the trunk of a squad.

If it'd been just TVs, he probably would have busted me, but VCRs were new and expensive. Everybody wanted one.

◇◇◇

I wasn't in on all the scores, but I sold all the shit.

I gave Fatboy keys so they could dump the merchandise in the garage. The TVs and VCRs were easy to get rid of, but they stole so much stuff, I couldn't move it fast enough. It seemed like every day there was something new. Soon the garage was packed. There were coat racks filled with ladies' dresses, piles of kids' winter coats, and stacks of shoeboxes. There were radios, silverware sets, pressure cookers, snow blowers, two refrigerators, a freezer, a washing machine, and four dozen black sombreros.

They came every day. Besides the TVs and VCRs, all the Zeniths, cops, and neighborhood people stuffed their trunks with lawn mowers, radios, and clothes. The ones without cars walked up and filled shopping carts. Once, when a load of women's shoes came in, I had a couple mothers show up pushing baby carriages. I had to put out chairs so they could sit and try on different sizes. It was like a regular department store.

I asked Jerry how the fuck he expected me to move the sombreros. He just shrugged and said that that was my problem.

It turned out he loved being a burglar. He chose riskier and riskier scores, and he suckered Fatboy into going along, because the way he figured it, Fatboy still owed him. Jerry even started bringing other cops along, whenever the Reverend wasn't available.

I told him the more people he brought in, the more likely we'd get caught, but he didn't care. Like gambling and women, he loved the rush. And like gambling and women, he just couldn't stop.

Charged with Mother's Murder

By James Thompson

A WEST SIDE MAN was charged Tuesday with hitting his mother with a baseball bat and then pushing her out of a sixth story window of the Oak Park Arms Hotel.

On Sunday, the body of Mrs. Maria Capelletti, of 1643 N. Lotus Avenue, was found on the sidewalk in front of the hotel's entrance.

Her son, Anthony, 22, turned himself in to police Monday evening.

Police said they couldn't provide a motive.

Just prior to her death, Mrs. Capalletti was busy preparing for her son's engagement party. She was standing on a chair hanging decorations when she was assaulted and shoved through the window.

"I can't believe it," said Mrs. Alice Bonczkowski, the Capallettis' next door neighbor. "I never saw any trouble between them. In fact, I talked to him Sunday night and asked him how he was. He seemed calm and cool."

CAPALLETTI WAS charged with two counts of murder, one for pushing his mother out of the window, and another for hitting her with a bat and pushing her out the window.

Merry Fucking Christmas

Christmas time is good for business. People spend money they don't have and, because a good chunk of drinkers don't have anybody, they spend it in the bar.

Every year I dragged the same old boxes of ornaments and lights out of the garage. On the side of each, in my mother's hand, was written: **XMAS!** I put the fake tree and ornament boxes on the pool table and put the rest on the bar.

The Skeletons and Railroad Bob wanted to put the tree together this year. Old Man Skeleton sat on a stool with the instructions in one hand and a beer in the other. Old Lady Skeleton and Railroad Bob stood with their hands full of plastic branches, waiting.

The old man held the directions under a bar light and read aloud: "On the stalk of each tree branch is a number. On the trunk of the tree there is a corresponding number for each branch. Working from the top down, place each branch in the corresponding number."

"Fuck that," Old Lady Skeleton said.

"Yeah," Railroad Bob said. "Fuck that."

"Follow the goddamn directions," Old Man Skeleton said.

"Any dumbshit can make rules," Railroad Bob said.

"If you don't do it right, it'll look like a fuckin' joke," Old Man Skeleton said.

"Artists should never be serious," Railroad Bob said. "Let's plant these fuckers."

Old Man Skeleton shook his head, threw the directions on the floor, turned around, and drank his beer. Old Lady Skeleton and Railroad Bob stuffed branches into notches until the box was empty. Instead of a triangle, the thing looked like a furry green blob. The added weight of ornaments and lights made it lean so much they had to tie to the wall.

On the back bar, I plugged in little snow-covered houses with twinkling lights, and I hung a cracked snowman on the mirror. I was in the middle of stringing the lights around the back bar when she came in.

Her grief always stopped me. It seemed to push through the door before she did, even. I somehow felt it ahead of the blast of bitter December air.

She walked right up to me, cold and forlorn. Her clothes were dirty. Her hair was a tangled mess. She didn't drink or smoke, but her skin was gray, and there were bags under her eyes. The grief pushed her shoulders toward the floor. Her hands remained buried in her thin black cloth overcoat. She looked like she'd been awake for days.

Mrs. Connolly had been coming in every few weeks asking about her son, Bill. He'd been missing since August of '77. One day, he left for work and never came back. He was nineteen.

None of us could make any sense of it. He was good people. He wasn't the kind to take off. He didn't drink too much, do dope, or gamble. Everybody liked him. He was the kind of kid who'd push-start a car for a stranger. He'd dropped out of high school, but it was only because his father died. He was the oldest, and his five brothers and sisters needed to eat, so he worked on the line at Brach's Candy and did side jobs painting houses. He worked hard and gave his mother his paycheck. The wildest thing he did was join a bowling team.

At first, we'd all looked for him. His picture had been on posters in the store windows, and taped to every lamp post in the neighborhood. We'd taken up a collection and offered a reward. Even Brach's chipped in. For weeks, I'd asked customers if they'd seen him, but it didn't take long before, like everybody else, I gave up and stopped asking.

Mrs. Connolly never gave up.

"Seen him?" she asked.

"No. Sorry," I said.

She nodded and turned. She walked out, crossed the street, and made her way to the next bar.

The rest of us didn't talk about it. It seemed like every day something happened. Bill Connolly was on a long list of people who got robbed, shot, stabbed, or beaten, or just plain disappeared. If we'd talked about them, we wouldn't have had time to talk about much else. Anyway, none of us could make any sense of it. Patients in a nuthouse don't talk about how everybody's crazy. What's the point?

Railroad Bob and Old Lady Skeleton sat down on stools and admired their tree.

"I like Christmas 'cause it's the only time bastards got a heart."

"Shut up," Old Man Skeleton said.

I'd set up a Christmas buffet with a crockpot of Italian beef, French bread, potato salad and chocolate chip cookies. The jukebox, the pool table, and bowling game were free. I told Fatboy to buy the regulars every other drink, and every third drink for the rest.

Every year on the night of the Christmas party, I allowed in the people I'd banned. There was Six Pack Sally, a street hustler who gave blowjobs for the price of, well, a six pack. There was Hatchet Mary, who'd done ten years for chopping her husband up and stuffing him in a freezer. There was Sailor John, who'd been kicked out of every branch of the service, and every bar on North Avenue.

Railroad Bob dyed his hair white and wore a Santa suit. That year, he'd convinced the Skeletons to dress up as elves. The three of them sat on stools sucking beer, chain smoking, and telling jokes.

"Hey, Bob," Old Lady Skeleton said. "What's it mean when a woman's got a man in her bed gaspin' and callin' her name?"

"What?"

"Means she didn't hold the pillow down long enough."

"Hey, Bob," Old Man Skeleton said, "Why'd God give us dicks?"

"Why?"

"So's we'd have a way to shut women up."

I told Fatboy that, if they were for real, all the kids wouldn't stand a fuckin' chance, especially not the ones on the 'naughty' list.

He snickered. "This Santa's *on* the naughty list."

The cops were bunched up near the pool table eating beef sandwiches and dripping the juice on my floor. The Zeniths sat in the front with their own plates. I poured shots of Jack for everybody.
The jukebox kept churning out "Jingle Bell Rock" until I couldn't take it anymore. I punched in some Brubeck.

Then a very drunk Dog Breath came in wearing his own Santa Suit.

"Hey! No interloper Santas," Railroad Bob said. With his wrinkly elves for backup, he stomped up to Dog Breath.

"We need a Santa that will bring good tidings," Dog Breath said.

"Damn you and your treachery."

"Come on!" Dog Breath grinned. "Where the fuck is your Christmas spirit?"

"Only the dead have seen war's end, motherfucker." Railroad Bob shoved Dog Breath, which sent him into the Zeniths. They pushed Dog Breath back into Railroad Bob, who toppled onto his elves. The elves then pushed Railroad Bob back onto Dog Breath.

Soon the two Santas were trading punches, their arms a blur of red velvet. Fatboy wanted to break it up, but I said they weren't hurting anybody but themselves. Besides, the crowd was enjoying the fight. Hatchet Mary and Six Pack Sally and Sailor John had elbowed their way up to the front rank and were hooting and hollering like the Bears had somehow made it to the Super Bowl. But the cops and Zeniths were eating it up, too.

Fists, cotton stuffing, and fake beards flew until Railroad Bob got the best of Dog Breath. Like a cowboy taking down a steer, he got the fat man into a headlock and wrangled him to the floor. Still, to his credit, Dog Breath kept sputtering, "Is this how you wish 'Merry Christmas?'"

Finally, I got bored and broke it up. I made the Santas shake hands, and bought them each a shot. Then they sat at the bar drinking with the elves. Dog Breath told the St. Anne's nurses that, if they'd sit on his lap, he'd give them something nice and hard for Christmas.

Then somebody brought in one of those inflatable fuck-toy party dolls filled with helium, and we celebrated Christ's birthday by batting it around the bar.

When the tremors in my hands started, I couldn't hold onto a bottle or punch the register. I waited for it to stop, but it didn't. I told Fatboy that I needed to go downstairs for some more Old Style. As I walked down the steps, I braced myself against the wall, but just as I reached the last few, I lost my balance, slammed against the opposite wall, and fell forward. My hands wouldn't let me break my fall. My body slammed against the concrete.

I just laid there. Above me, I heard the feet stomp back and forth, and the cops were laughing, and the Zeniths started singing: *We're in the mood for Sally simply because she's easy, simply because she's easy, and she fucks for free.* I swear I could hear Six Pack Sally's muffled laughter through the floorboards. She said something like: I never gave it away in my life, and I ain't startin' with you bastards.

Even after the pain, tremors, and dizziness stopped, I didn't get up right away. It was my goddamn carnival, and I stayed there listening, because I knew that, one day, Huntington's would take it all, even the memories.

I did get up eventually, but didn't head back behind the bar. I knew they'd ask where I'd been, why I'd been gone so long. I didn't want to deal with it. So I brought a beer out to the Reverend.

The Reverend didn't come to the party. Except to use the john or come looking for Jerry, he never came in the bar at all, and that night was no different. But Jerry had asked him to keep an eye on things, so he was sitting in his squad in the alley.

He wasn't a big drinker. A couple of times a night, I'd run a beer out to him, but that was about it. That night when I came out, he had a book and was leaning under the squad's dome light. He had a pair of reading glasses perched on his nose. My feet crunched a little on the snow, but he didn't look up. When I tapped on the window, he finally jumped a little and snapped his head. He rolled down the window and snatched the beer from me.

"Cold," I said.

"Yeah," he said.

"Wanna come in?"

"Have I ever?"

"No."

"Why start now?"

"Why not?" I asked.

He looked at me like I'd asked why he didn't eat glass. "Would you ask if I didn't have a badge?"

"Sure."

"White people always say that shit."

"We're not all like that."

He smirked and threw his book and glasses on the dash. "I was sixteen. Going to a Sox game. I was late. Had to run. This old white man gave me the look and says, 'Why you runnin'?' The cops came outta nowhere. They asked me why I was runnin' too and I told 'em, but they shoved me in the car anyway."

"I tried to get out of it. I was scared about what my parents would do. The boy preacher picked up by the police? But when they took me over to 47th, that's when I got really scared."

"They got these white men outta tavern. Beat me until I was throwin' up blood. The worst part was the begging. I told those cocksuckers I was sorry. For what? Goin' to a fucking baseball game?"

"They left me on the sidewalk. Then this man came and wiped the blood from my face. He helped me up. I didn't look at him. I just wanted to get the fuck out of there. 'We're not all like that,' he said."

"So, you ain't all like that, but there sure as hell enough of you who are. And when there's a room full of you motherfuckers, sooner or later, one of you is gonna do somethin' to piss me off. Well, I ain't sixteen any more, and nowadays I got a gun. So it's better if I stay in the car. Merry fucking Christmas."

He rolled up the window, put on his glasses and went back to reading his book.

I didn't say anything. I walked back into the bar. I believed his story, pretty much, but still I couldn't help thinking: What did you expect?

He was right about one thing, though: if he wasn't a cop, I'd never have asked him in. I had enough trouble as it was.

I was just about to head back inside when I noticed a sliver of light coming from under the garage door. At first, I was pissed at myself for leaving it on, but when I opened the door, I saw water on the floor and footprints leading to the fridge, and I knew it hadn't been me. Fatboy, maybe?

Inside in the cold light I saw: ground beef, pork chops, steaks, ham, turkeys, provolone, Swiss.

Back in the bar, the party was still in full swing. Fatboy was running around like a crazy man. He gave me a look like: Where the hell have you been? But I gave him one like: We need to talk.

He put three Old Styles on the counter, grabbed the money, and walked over.

"What's that in the garage fridge?" I asked.

He cupped his hand and talked in my ear: "Van's."

"Van's?" Jesus. I shook my head, disgusted.

"Last night. Jerry and me. Easy score."

It was an easy score, but a really dumb one.

"Look, we..." I started, but right then, the door swung open and a drunk Jerry stomped in. He grabbed onto shoulders and climbed up on a stool. He reached over for the TV and turned the dial. He looked at us with a strange demented gleam.

"What the fuck are you changing the channel for?" Santa Skeleton yelled.

"Fuckin' ten o'clock news!" Jerry yelled back.

"Fuck the fuckin' news!"

"You need to see this shit," Jerry said as the pictures came on.

There are times when everybody in a bar shuts the hell up. This was one of those times.

We were used to violence. We all knew somebody who'd been shot or stabbed. As kids, when we were bored, we'd fight each other for fun. But that night on that screen we saw something that got to us, even. Four men, each holding the corner of a sheet-covered stretcher, walked out of a ranch house near O'Hare. They put the stretcher in a van and then turned around and went back for another. They looked tired, like soldiers retreating.

The Santas and the elves stood there, mouths wide open. One of the St. Anne's nurses put her hand to her face. The cops and Zeniths looked up at the screen like it was a pulpit. Even Hatchet Mary stopped drinking. Nobody said anything. Nobody, except Jerry.

"Look at this shit!" he said. "Degenerate faggot. What's wrong with people these days?"

Gacy had been doing it for years. He was a construction contractor who'd conned many by promising work. Other times, he impersonated a cop and forced them into his car. He'd drugged, raped, and strangled them. He'd stuffed them in the crawlspace of the house. To keep the stench down, he'd covered them with lime. We were told that, when he ran out of room, he dumped more of them off the I-55 Bridge and into the Des Plaines River.

Names poured out of the screen. They were young, most just boys. Many were like Bill Connolly, average guys who one day, for no reason, disappeared.

I waited to hear Bill's name. In a way, I wanted to hear it. I wanted it to be over for Mrs. Connolly. But it never came. She'd have to go on searching the streets, forced to ask people like me if we'd seen her son, wondering why God had chosen to take him away without even letting him say goodbye.

When the story ended, the crowd mumbled to each other for a couple of minutes and then went back to drinking. I turned off the TV and turned up the jukebox.

Fatboy threw glasses into soapy water, emptied ashtrays, and wiped down the bar. Then, with nothing left to clean, he stood frozen in front of the register. He ignored the hand waving and shouts of drunks. He stared through them. I nudged him and told him to take a break. He nodded and went outside.

◇◇◇

The party went on. Of course it wasn't the same after that, but it was like everyone drank even harder, to pretend like it was.

When it was all over, Fatboy was back at work, cleaning up puke and broken glass. I pulled him aside. "Look, Van's..."

"Jerry's idea," he said.

"I don't give a fuck who's idea it was. Nobody gives a shit when you rip off a big place like Sears, or some business run by an asshole, but Van's..." We both knew what the store meant to everyone. It was just a few blocks from the tavern. Tim and Mary Murphy knew everybody by name. Their family had owned Van's for years. Their prices were good and they gave easy credit. Their kids worked at the store and went to St. Lucy's. Any day of the week you could find something sponsored by Van's. They paid for little league, bowling, softball, and gave to the North Austin Boy's Club. They were real, honest to God, good people. I never heard of them scamming anybody. In fact, the whole damn family volunteered for charities. And, if that wasn't bad enough, Mary was the head of the Altar and Rosary Society and, every Sunday, Tim was a fucking usher.

"Nobody saw us," Fatboy said.

"Don't matter."

"I'm serious. Nobody saw us."

"Jesus Christ, it don't matter! Everybody's gonna know anyway! I'm sellin' stolen shit out the back and you assholes ripped off the one goddamn place everybody loves. It'd be better if ya'd snatched wheelchairs from cripples."

"Jerry's idea," he said again.

"Ya coulda told him no."

"Couldn't."

"Well ya better start. He's gonna get us pinched."

I started cleaning up the food. I got hungry and wanted a sandwich, but there was nothing left in the Italian beef tray, just juice and scraps. I stirred it around with the tongs but couldn't find anything bigger than a dime.

Fuck it, I said at last. I went out to the garage and opened the fridge and made myself a ham and cheese.

The next day, I called a guy I knew on the North Side and got rid of everything in there. I told Jerry I'd sell off the rest of the stuff and then I was done. He didn't like it, but I didn't give a shit. I wasn't going to jail for anybody.

Warwick out of TV business

WARWICK ELECTRONICS INC. announced Tuesday it will sell its television manufacturing division to Sanyo.

Once the main supplier of Sears' Silvertone televisions, Warwick cited the retailer's transition to foreign manufacturers as its motivation for selling. The company's television division saw a 60 percent decline in revenue in 1977, with more losses forecast for 1978.

The acquisition of Warwick's Forest City, Arkansas plant will provide Sanyo the ability to manufacture televisions in the United States.

Sanyo will purchase the 57 percent share of the division currently held by Whirlpool Corporation. Sears will keep the 25 percent it currently holds. The remaining shares will be channeled into the Sanyo's newly-formed US subsidiary.

Warwick will continue to manufacture electronic organs under its Thomas International Division.

Jousters 4 Ever

I came to the back door and knocked and stood shivering in the cold, waiting.

When she finally answered, she grabbed my hand and pulled me in, but she didn't kiss me. Instead, she pointed to what had to be at least twenty cases of Old Style stacked up on her back porch. She asked me if I knew where they'd come from and I told her I didn't.

"You're full of shit," she said.

She pulled me out to the garage. In the middle of the floor, there were two mounds with green tarps over them. She yanked them off. Under one, there were sets of golf clubs. Under the other were three snow blowers.

She stood there and stared at me. Her arms were folded and her face was tight. Her breath made cold little clouds. She asked me what the fuck was going on and I said I didn't know.

But she wasn't stupid. In fact, she was smarter than most.

She knew I was lying. She said Fatboy, Jerry, and her father had lied to her so many times it was the truth that surprised her. "All the times I asked you about

Jerry," she said, "I knew you lied because you didn't want to hurt me. So I played the fool. It made it easier. But it's always pissed me off. Did you really think that I was that stupid? After everything, did you really think you had to protect me?"

She'd knew we'd been selling out of the tavern, and she knew the stuff in the garage meant Jerry was part of it.

"I need him. He may be an asshole, but I need him. Out here, not in jail."

"Talk to him then. I tried already. This was his idea. This was his doing."

"This is all of you. This is going to put my husband in jail. This is going to send my brother back, the way you're doing this."

"Your husband." I shook my head.

She didn't like that.

"Look, I'm sorry," I said at last. "I'm sorry about all of this. This isn't what I wanted." But when I moved closer, she backed away.

"Don't think I don't know about my husband. I know about his women. I know about the money and where it goes. I knew about it before we got married. But he did marry me. He stepped up."

Then she told me something I didn't need to be told. She said Jerry was an asshole, but loyal in his own ways, in ways I wasn't. Loyalty meant everything to him.

◇◇◇

Jerry and I were nine. It was July and it was so hot that the tar in the sidewalk cracks stuck to the bottom of our sneakers. We were bored. We'd already played softball, sprayed cars with an open fire hydrant, pitched pennies, and jammed parking meters with slugs. We needed something else to do.

We'd heard about putting pennies on the tracks. We went to the rail yard under the Central Avenue Bridge. We didn't have shirts on and the sun burned our backs red as we made our way to the middle of the bridge.

There was a gate. It was unlocked. There was a steel stairway. Jerry opened the gate. I didn't want to go. I got scared. I'd never gone down to the tracks. Jerry called me a pussy. He told me that if I didn't do it, he'd tell everybody I'd chickened out.

I followed him. We trotted down the steps to a cement island in the middle of the tracks. We stopped for a minute. In the distance we could see the skyline. In the heat the buildings seemed to sway.

Jerry pulled my arm. We ran over the tracks until we reached the outbound side. We knelt down next to the tracks and lined up our pennies on the rails. Then we ran to the siding and hid between some parked boxcars.

Soon we saw the train. I'd never been so close to one before. The ground shook. Boxcars banged and swayed. Stones spit. The whistle blasted. I clamped my hands over my ears. The thing went on forever. I was nothing.

When the last car passed, we waited until we could barely make out the train. Then we ran over to see what it had done to our pennies. Lincoln's head looked like one of those carnival mirrors. Jerry said he looked like Ming the Merciless from the Flash Gordon show.

We were so caught up in it that we didn't see the man until he was just a few feet from us.

He was taller than my father, but skinnier. He wore dirty jeans, gloves, and a sweaty white T-shirt. The cigarette between his lips bounced. There was a tattoo on his forearm of a knight's helmet. Under it was written **Jousters 4 Ever**. He told us to stay put. The fear made me like a fence post, but then Jerry pulled my arm and we ran across the tracks toward the stairway.

I tried to keep up, but Jerry was faster. The man tried to grab me by the neck, but it was slick with sweat. He caught hold of my arm, and squeezed it tight. He yanked me toward the boxcars. I heard myself crying. He told me to shut up.

I couldn't see where Jerry had gone. I hated him for leaving me.

The man dragged me between two cars. He bent down and looked at me. "What the fuck were you doin'?" he said. I tried to say something, but the fear wouldn't let me. He said he was sick of kids coming down onto the tracks.

He slapped me in the face and I felt rage that made me want to grind his face into the cinders and kick him until he was a bloody heap. But like every bastard with a bit of power, he made damn sure I knew he was strong and I was weak.

"What the fuck were you doin'?" he said. "You a stupid motherfucker? Huh? Well, are ya?" And I shook my head. And I guess he took my silence as me being a smartass. He told me that it would be the last time I'd ever be stupid enough to fuck around on the tracks.

When the cigarette hit my chest, I heard myself scream. I'd had my share of injuries. But I'd never felt pain like that. My skin sizzled and I could smell my flesh burn.

He told me to shut up. When he was done, he told me he had to do it one more time, so I'd learn my lesson.

I heard myself beg him not to. I heard myself swear that I'd never do it again. "Don't," I said.

But before he could bury the ember back into my skin, the board came down on his skull, a hard smack. Jerry.

The man let go of my arm. I had to get out of the way when he fell. He hit his face against the side of the boxcar. I stood there staring at him. The blood was pouring out of his head. Jerry dropped the board. "Run," he said.

We must have stopped somewhere along the way, but it seemed like we ran all the way back to the neighborhood. We went to Jerry's basement and put cold water on the burn.

I wasn't supposed to go to the trains. I had to hide it from my parents. Jerry took one of his T-shirts from a pile of dirty laundry and gave it to me.

After that, I was worried he was going to tell the neighborhood he'd had to save me, that he'd heard me screaming like a little bitch, like a sissy. But he never told a soul.

Rita, Fatboy, and I sat around the kitchen table. Fatboy looked like a kid getting ready for a smack. He had his arms crossed and was looking down. She was leaning over the table and had her finger pointed in my face.

"My brother is not going back," she said.

"It's not his fault." Fatboy talked into his chest. "I'm a big boy. I made my own decisions."

Rita sat back. She looked at her brother and then at me. Then she shook her head. "Men. If you had a fuckin' brain between ya, you'd take it out and play with it."

I told her I'd leave if she wanted me to. I was hoping that she'd tell me to go. It wasn't so much her anger that bothered me. It was that I was now added to the long list of people who'd let her down. I couldn't take the disappointed looks she threw at me.

But she told me to stay. "You're not gettin' off for this one," she said.

There was only an hour left before her kids would be home, so she let loose on her brother. "You're an idiot," she said. "Are you usin'?"

He said he wasn't. And then he told her something that floored me. He said he'd met this guy, Joe, in prison. He'd been hoping for a steady job so maybe the two of them could get a place together when Joe got out. But then he found out that there'd be no job. So, when I made the offer, he'd grabbed it. "When Joe gets out there'll be something for us," he said.

Until then, I'd just been sitting there drinking coffee, listening to a brother and sister argue, and dodging the occasional look from Rita. But when Fatboy said he was in love with a man, the words spit from my mouth before I could stop them. "You're queer?"

Rita looked up at the ceiling and laughed. "Have you ever seen my brother with a woman?"

Fatboy just sat there. He didn't even look at me.

"Sure," I said, although I wasn't. "There's that photo on the mantel of him with whats-her-name...that girl he took to prom."

"Of course he took a girl to the fucking prom. He'd have gotten his ass kicked if he didn't."

I really didn't know what to say. "Jerry know?"

"Are you crazy?"

"Wow," I said. "Queer."

"Look who's talkin'," she said. "You're screwing your best friend's wife."

Finally Fatboy looked at me. "You're sleepin' with my sister?"

Rita put her head back, closed her eyes, and said: "Un-fucking believable."

"What?"

"The three men closest to me. So goddamn blind! All of you."

But we weren't blind. We were shell-shocked. Our days were filled with punches thrown. We didn't plan. We reacted.

She didn't say anything for a while. She sat back in her chair, closed her eyes, and took deep breaths. "Currency exchange," she said at last.

"What?" Now I was really confused.

"If you want to take stupid fuckin' risks, you might as well do it for a big reward. Tide you over for a bit. Get a lot of cash and stop doing stupid robberies. Best way to do that would be to hit a currency exchange."

"How do you figure?" I asked.

"They got lots of cash."

"So do banks."

"Yeah, but a currency exchange, they usually keep it in a safe instead of a vault. With a few guys and the right equipment, you could roll a safe right out. Plus, they carry small bills. All of it goes in your pockets."

It was a good idea and I ran with it. Fatboy and I talked about possible targets, the equipment needed, and the best time to hit one. It didn't take long before I fooled myself into thinking I'd come up with the idea, that she had nothing to do with it. I had to. I needed her to be better than me.

◇◇◇

That night, I found myself back at the bar, going through the normal motions.

Gin and Tonic Doc sat at the bar same as always, wearing his uniform of tweed jacket, white shirt, and bow tie. The Skeletons were looking into each other's eyes and singing *Are You Lonesome Tonight*. Railroad Bob was in the Men's Room again. Once in a while he'd holler "Holy Hell!" Or Jesus Fucking Christ!" I asked him if he was okay. "Questionable," he said.

Everything seemed as usual. Still, I couldn't get the news of Fatboy being queer out of my mind. If it was so obvious, why didn't I see it? I poured myself a beer and sat next to Doc. He was the only other one I knew for sure about. I asked him if he noticed anything different about Fatboy. "He's queer," he said.

"How do you know?"

He gave me a look like I was missing the obvious. "He has sex with men."

I gave him a look like: I'm not stupid. "What, like he fooled around with you?"

"No."

"Well what makes him a fag, then? Not everyone who's done something stupid is that way. I've seen you drag guys out of the bar. I know you end up giving 'em blowjobs in parked cars, all that sick shit. But those guys aren't fags. They're drunk."

"You ever been drunk?"

"Yeah."

"Ever fuck a man?"

"No."

"Ever been fucked by a man?"

"No."

"Ever suck a cock?"

"Hell no."

"Ever get your cock sucked by a man?"

"No."

"Straight men don't have sex with men."

He told me that the drunks who climbed into the back of cars with him were as queer as he was, but they just couldn't face it. They did everything they could to bury it. They got married. They had kids. They were churchgoers and coached football. When they were with their friends, they told jokes about women with big tits and always laughed the loudest. "But, no matter how much they try to bury it, when they get drunk, down come the pants," he said. "I never have to go to them. They always come to me."

"Fatboy never goes with you," I said.

"He never leaves with anybody. When the jokes are told, he just smirks, shakes his head, and walks away. He's no prude. He's bored. Plenty of women flirt with him. He's polite and sometimes he even reciprocates a little, but phone numbers are never exchanged. Dates are never made. One night, I watched this drunk, horny nurse drool over him all night. When he went to the men's room, she followed him. She wasn't in there more than a few seconds. He walked her back to her friends and bought them a round. But the thing is, sometimes, when there's a lull in business and he's sure no one is looking, he looks over the crowd and chooses one man. And he looks at that man like you look at Rita. He's queer. He's just not a slut. Other guys are. Guys you wouldn't suspect."

"Uh huh," I said.

"I'll prove it to you," he said.

"Sure." I still didn't quite believe it.

◇◇◇

Later that night, this retired cop named Jim McCarthy came in. He was a little bastard who acted like he was still a cop. He kept a ring of keys on his belt and carried a gun. He was the same age as some of the other ones, but had to retire early when he was shot by a robbery suspect. Unfortunately, it was a black guy who blew a hole in him.

Most people in the neighborhood had no love for black people, but this guy was all for burning crosses and stringing them up. There were rumors that he was involved with some Nazi group on the South Side. When he wasn't spewing shit about black people, he was rambling on about how Jews were all part of an international banking conspiracy that was destroying the country.

Usually, I didn't put up with nuts, but he didn't come in too often, and the older cops he'd worked with remembered when he wasn't such an asshole. So that night, as always, they listened to his stories of the old days, bought him drinks, and shot pool with him. One of them gave him a sombrero that he wore all night. It was finally getting a little busy, but that sombrero stood out, and I watched it move through the crowd.

It took a few hours, and a few drinks, but I watched the sombrero get closer and closer until McCarthy took a seat next to Doc. McCarthy didn't look at him. In fact, he tried to look away, but sometimes he'd steal a glance in the mirror, like he couldn't help himself. He did it several times, and finally he didn't look away and locked eyes with Doc. That's when I saw Doc's hand leave the bar and McCarthy's jaw drop. Then Doc got up, looked at me, winked, and walked out the door with the sombrero-wearing asshole following him like a kid follows the ice cream man.

About a half hour later, Doc came back in without Sombrero Boy and took his usual seat. I fixed him a gin and tonic and put it in front of him.

"See?" he said.

I didn't say nothing. What could I say? Until then, I thought I was street smart. I thought I knew all about the neighborhood and the people in it. I thought I could read people, but now I was wondering.

And I couldn't help but think about our little crew. Me, Jerry, Fatboy and the Reverend. I thought I knew them, but I'd been coming to realize more and more that Jerry was a degenerate. And now with this with Fatboy...hell, it almost seemed like the Reverend was the normal one out of the bunch, which was disturbing in its own right. But maybe Rita was right. Maybe I was blind.

She was right about one thing for sure, though: the currency exchange. While I needed to get out, it was dumb to take all those risks if there wasn't at least going to be a big reward at the end. And I needed that. I couldn't let Van's be the end of it. Something good had to come out of all this.

We're Americans

Jerry and I sat in my living room drinking Old Style and watching the Bears lose.

Soldier Field was designed to look like a Roman stadium, but Bears' fans sure as hell didn't act like any Romans I'd ever read about. By the fourth quarter, they were so drunk they killed time by throwing snowballs at the players. Every once in a while, one would hit a helmet, snow would splatter, and the crowd would cheer.

Fatboy'd told me we'd need at least four guys to get the safe out. He didn't want cops in on the score, especially Jerry. He said we needed professionals. He had people in mind, but I told him I wouldn't do it without Jerry.

Most of the time, he was a real asshole, but Rita was right: Jerry was loyal. And it wasn't just when we were kids. When we found my parents, he tried to save them. And when I was a drunk, he'd done his best to save me too.

◇◇◇

It'd been rough after my parents died. I avoided everybody. I drew the curtains and stayed in the apartment as much as I could. I had food delivered and did my best to drink up the inventory. Most times, I'd wake up on the floor, surrounded by empty bottles, greasy pizza boxes, and half-eaten bags of chips. I'd lay there in the dark apartment and listen to cockroaches running over cardboard, coming to get their share.

Every time Jerry came by, I'd tell him I was fine and I'd be opening up soon. When I'd say it, I'd mean it, but when I'd get down to the bar, I couldn't handle the thought of pushing booze and dealing with drunks. Without my mother, it was too much. I'd grab a bottle, turn around, and go back upstairs.

Then one morning, Jerry pounded on my door until I answered. He took my keys from me. He said he wasn't going to listen to my bullshit anymore, and even if I didn't give a shit about the tavern, he did. Next thing I knew, he was running my bar for me in his off hours. He made it into a cop bar. He brought in all of his friends.

One night, after finishing off a bottle of scotch, I decided it was the perfect time to take a shower. Just as I got fully soaped up, I lost my balance, fell backwards out of the tub, and banged my head against the wall. I hit the floor hard, and everything went black.

When I woke up the next morning, the pain shot through me, and I wondered if I could ever get up. I crawled out of the bathroom. I laid flat on my back. I stared at the ceiling. I'd seen a lot of street drunks, and I knew it wouldn't take much until I was right down there with them, hustling quarters and waking up in alleys. With my luck, I'd have lasted years living like that.

It hurt like hell, but I turned over and got on all fours. I grabbed a chair for support and got to my feet. I put on some clothes and went downstairs. I took the keys from Jerry, and took over the business again. He never asked me for a dime, and we never talked about what he'd done for me.

◇◇◇

Had I been thinking only about recent events, I probably would have cut Jerry out of the currency exchange. But you can't ignore personal history. So even though I had some doubts, I figured I had to include him.

When I told him, he was like a dog with a piece of meat. I could tell everything else didn't matter to him now: the Bears game, Rita, nothing. He leaned back in his chair and smiled. His legs were shaking.

"How much?" He couldn't hide the eagerness from his voice.

"Right one, right time, twenty maybe thirty grand," I said.

"Fucking great."

"You're really into this."

"Nothing like it," he said. "I get scared, but that's part of it. And it's not what I'm boostin'. It could be anything. Every time, it feels so good. Sometimes, I think it's better than fuckin'."

"If the money's right, we'll need to be cool. This'll be the last."

"No problem."

"You sure?"

"Not a idiot."

"Okay."

"When?"

"Don't know. Gotta find the right one."

Watching him, it dawned on me that it didn't matter if we got the right one, or how much money we took. He'd never stop. He couldn't.

I knew right then he'd fuck it up. I knew right then I shouldn't have told him. And part of me knew it still wasn't too late. I could have started making up some excuse to scrap the whole thing, or drag my feet, but I didn't. So I drank beer, watched snowballs fly, and hated him for debts I could never repay.

Currency exchanges are banks for the poor. It's where money orders are bought and bills are paid. Best of all, it's where paychecks are cashed. Finding one wasn't hard. They were always on busy corners near bus or El stops, but finding the right one was another story.

Fatboy and I rode around for hours, just looking. He had bought this beat up Impala. People talk about their car being a deathtrap, but Fatboy's really was. Rust had rotted through the trunk and exhaust pipe. Fumes came through the speaker vent. They were so bad we had to keep the back windows open. The hood was held down with a lock and chain that banged against the grill. There was a hole on the passenger side. The only thing keeping my feet from hitting the street was a few layers of carpet remnants that he'd thrown over it. That was useful, though. I'd brought along a six pack and, when we'd finish a can, I'd pick up the carpet and drop it into the street. If I angled it just right, the back wheel would crush it.

The Impala had an eight track. Fatboy had one tape. After listening to "Black Magic Woman" ten times, I couldn't take it anymore and switched it off. We made small talk, but how many times can you talk about how shitty the Bears are? So I asked him what prison was like.

Usually guys who do time don't talk much about it. But I guess because we each had something on the other, he figured he could let loose.

"It was shit," he said. "Got raped early on. I was dope sick. He was stronger. Nothing I could do. After that was when I met Joe. He taught me the only thing the animals respect is what you're willing to do. You don't have to win every fight, but they have to know, no matter what happens, you'll hurt 'em. Most of 'em are cowards. Pretty soon they leave you alone."

He said that, a few years before, Joe had shoved a shiv into a guy's neck in front of the entire yard and, for that, he'd gotten another seven years. And, with a pride in his voice that I don't think I've ever heard in anyone else, Fatboy said, "After that, nobody touched him unless he want to be touched."

Fatboy said Joe never tried to force him into anything. "He wanted it to be my decision," he said. "He protected me, helped me get off dope, and schooled me on what I needed to do." Being with Joe meant he was protected, but Joe convinced him that that was a problem.

In Joliet, although Joe was feared, anybody could be gotten rid of. "Most of the time," Fatboy said, "you don't even see it comin'." He told me of people with bulging eyes found shaking on concrete floors with froth coming from their mouths. He said one guy switched on a bulb and was blinded by lighter fluid and cooking oil. "His face was all burned up," he said. "If Joe was gone, either I'd have to get the guy who raped me, or I'd get passed around."

They knew they had to send a message, but not add more time. The message had to be strong enough that no one would ever think Fatboy was an easy target again. Fatboy wanted to kill him, but Joe convinced him it'd be a bad idea. "He said, if I killed him, I'd never be the same. I saw the pain in his face. I knew it was true."

So they came up with a plan. "On Wednesdays," he said, "he'd leave his job in the cafeteria early for a AA meeting. We paid a maintenance guy to forget a steel pipe. There was a blind spot on the tier. At first, when he came around the corner and saw me, he was shocked. He stood there for a second, but then he smirked and looked at me like I was nothing. He tried to go around. I saw red. I swung. He tried to grab the pipe, but I was too quick. Every time, I swung that thing as hard as I could. When I stopped, he was on the floor cryin'. It was this pitiful, weak cry. When I was a kid, I was standin' in front of my dad's house. This girl came along with a dog. I guess the dog saw something, 'cause he ran into the street. This car clipped him. He spun around once before hitting the street. The blood poured out of him. He lifted his head and made that same kinda cry. The girl cried too. I felt sorry for her and the dog. I didn't feel sorry for him. After he raped me, he didn't give a shit. He just pulled up his pants and walked away. So, when I was done beatin' the shit outta him, I dropped the pipe and did the same thing. After that, nobody fucked with me. Joe and me watched out for each other."

I didn't say anything, not right then.

"So, yeah," Fatboy continued. "That's what prison was like."

"OK," I said. "Ya wanna another beer?"

"Yeah."

He was Rita's brother. But of course this reminded me of the rumors about him killing the old man. I wanted to believe what he'd said about being in the dope house that day. I tried to push it out of my head, but the way he described swinging that pipe kept coming back.

I turned the tape back on and blasted "Oye Como Va" until it was the only thing in my brain.

At last, we found it.

It was across from Tony's House of Beef, so we went in there to keep an eye on everything and make sure. But I knew we'd found it.

Tony's looked like somebody'd ate the Italian flag and threw it up. The chairs were green, tables red, and counters white. There were framed pictures with autographs. In the middle of them was one of Frank Sinatra with the note, "Nice beef. Frank." Fatboy and I sat at a counter, eating sandwiches, drinking pop, and staring across the icy winter street at the currency exchange.

It was south of the neighborhood, on the corner of Roosevelt and Central. It was wedged between the Cicero bars and the Western Electric plant. There was a big display window and a yellow sign that read: **CHECKS CASHED**. The roof was covered in razor wire.

At shift change, a big chunk of workers went in. We went with them. The walls were tiled and had charts with fees. There were two cashier windows covered with bulletproof glass. Above each were the signs: **NO PERSONAL CHECKS** and **TWO IDs REQUIRED FOR ALL PAYCHECKS** and **THIS MEANS YOU**.

Around the cashier windows was a wall of sheet metal. There was a curved steel slot at the bottom of each window just big enough to slip paperwork and cash through. In the center of each window was a metal circle with slots. Next to one of the windows was a steel door with two deadbolts. Somebody'd scratched **ASSHOLE** into it, with an arrow pointing to the cashier.

The cashier had his hair slicked back and wore reading glasses slid halfway down his nose. He had an old manual adding machine. He punched in numbers and pulled the crank. He pulled that thing so hard, you'd have thought it'd told him to go fuck his mother. He chain-smoked cigarettes and squashed the butts into a beanbag ashtray. Behind him was a safe that looked like it could fit through a doorway.

We had two people in front of us: an old man, and a woman with a kid. The woman paid her bills, gave the kid's arm a yank, and walked out the door. The old man shoved his check through the slot. The cashier looked at the check and then at him. He pushed the check back through the slot.

"ID," he said.

"You know me."

"ID."

"Sonuvabitch."

The old man snatched up the check and walked out. When it was Fatboy's turn, he bought some bus tokens and walked out too. I bought a book of stamps and did the same. The cashier was an asshole and I was glad. It made it easier to do what we were gonna do.

As we walked back to the car, Fatboy said we'd never get in through the front. "With that display window, anybody passing by will see us," he said. "We could go through the roof, but it'd be a bitch. We'd have to cut through all that razor wire and the roof. Noisy."

We waited in the car until after asshole closed up. Then we drove around back. The alley was choked with snow and ice. But there was enough room to squeeze in a van. We could back it in and work out of sight. There was no alarm, but there was a thick, solid door with two bolt locks. Fatboy said that he was sure on the other side of it were at least two metal bars. "But that don't matter," he laughed.

"Why?" I said.

"It's a fuckin' wood door."

◇◇◇

We headed back down Central toward the neighborhood. Everything was winter. We passed blocks of apartment buildings, two flats, and bungalows that used to be stuffed with Italians, Poles, Germans and Irish. Years before they'd jumped at offers from panic peddlers to sell before *they* invaded the neighborhood.

People say sex sells. Fuck that. Fear kicks sex's ass every goddamn time. It makes them give up their social clubs, churches and schools. It makes them burn down family businesses for insurance money. It makes them sell their brick bungalows for three quarters what they're worth. It makes them run for it down the Eisenhower, those six lanes of concrete that Daley cut through Columbus Park like a scar. It makes them buy overpriced shitty frame ranch houses on streets with sidewalks that lead to nothing. It makes them spend the rest of their lives driving twenty minutes just to get a fucking loaf of bread.

It had happened long ago in other neighborhoods, and it had started in ours. And I knew it wouldn't be long before everybody I knew was gone. I figured five years at the most, but it didn't matter. I'd leave them before they'd leave me.

Right before the Lake Street El, we passed the Central YMCA. Fatboy said that it was where he'd learned to swim.

"Every kid in the neighborhood learned there," I told him.

"The neighborhood," he said. He said nothing else for a while, just stared out at the bitter winter city.

The side streets were full of snow and slush, but Central had been plowed and salted. We rolled through green after green, and finally when we stopped for a red light at Division, he spoke again: "Where'd we learn this?"

"What?" I said.

"Takin' advantage of people. Why's it come so easy?"

The light changed. I watched the bricks of the buildings become a sheet of red. "We're Americans," I said.

Body Found in West Side Sewer

By James Thompson

Through fingerprint analysis, the body of a man found in a West Side sewer last week was identified as Dominick Fioretti, 35, of 2626 74th Ct., Elmwood Park.

The Cook County Coroner's Office says the victim had been shot twice, and his throat had been cut. His body was then wrapped in a tarp and bound with duct tape.

A group of boys playing street hockey made the discovery when they lost a puck in a sewer grating. In attempt to retrieve it, they pried the cover off and saw the body.

One of the boys informed his father, who called the police.

The body was found in an alley behind 1872 N. Luna. A rail yard runs adjacent to the alley.

A neighbor, who requested anonymity, said that several weeks ago, from her bedroom window, she saw a late model, tan car pull up with its lights off. The car stayed there for several minutes.

Suspicious, she called the police, but, by the time they arrived, the car had driven off.

In addition to fingerprints, the body was identified by a signet ring with the initials "DF." The ring was verified as Mr. Fioretti's by his brother. The victim also wore an expensive diamond watch and gold crucifix.

The police have ruled out robbery as a motive.

Mr. Fioretti had a long history of arrests and was a known associate of Chicago's organized crime syndicate.

The police have not released the names of any suspects.

Gas Money

In the bar business, when a blizzard hits, it's like getting an extra Friday night. People can't go to work, kids can't go to school, and everybody's stuck in the house. After a few hours of togetherness, Daddy and Mommy start getting a bit squirrelly. Then Daddy gets the hell out of the house, hopefully before somebody gets smacked, stabbed, or shot. And the first place he thinks about going is the tavern.

That's what happened that January. There'd been snow already, and the city got hit with so much more of it that nobody could move. The sidewalks were covered with mounds of it. The TV news showed buses, trucks, and cars stalled out and abandoned in the middle of streets, like toys in a sandbox.

I wanted to be ready. When Daddy decided to get out of the house, I wanted him to know the journey was worth it. I lit the place up. I made sure Donald shoveled and salted the sidewalk. With duct tape, I slapped a big **OPEN** sign onto the glass block. I stocked the coolers, filled the ice bins, and made sure there was plenty of change in the till.

Then I had an idea. I went down in the basement and found two bottles of tequila. My mother bought them to try to get ahead of a trend that never happened. I grabbed some party streamers, paper plates, napkins, and tablecloths left over from Christmas. Then I went over to Van's and bought stuff for tortilla chips and stuff for tacos. I put out bowls of chips on the bar and cooked up the tacos. Then I stacked up the sombreros behind the bar.

That night, we had a Cinco de Mayo party. It didn't matter that it was winter. Nobody knew what the hell Cinco de Mayo was, but I knew that if I gave them a tequila shot with every sombrero they bought, they'd go for it. I also knew that, because of the blizzard, there was nowhere to go for food.

By eight o'clock, I had a full bar. There were melting puddles of slush and snow, and coats were flung everywhere, but I didn't care. Every once in a while, someone's kid would come in with a message from Mommy to come home. Daddy'd send them off with a bag of chips, a can of pop, and return message of *go to hell*. By nine, they were more than willing to pay me a buck for a taco. By ten most of them were so drunk they paid me five for a sombrero. The only thing on the jukebox to go along with tequila, sombreros, and tacos was "Feliz Navidad." Every half hour I'd play it and they'd sing along.

I gotta admit, it was nice for a bit. It felt like old times. For a few hours, I got to forget everything. I could forget about the currency exchange, and Jerry and Fatboy and the Reverend, and what we were going to have to do.

Things were going great until Reynolds walked in. Unlike me, the owner of his regular bar couldn't open, because he didn't live in the neighborhood. So Reynolds walked the six blocks to mine. He was an old man and shouldn't have risked it, but that's the pull of the bottle and lust.

Reynolds had on a navy pea coat covered with a layer of snow. He took it off, shook it, and put it over his arm. You could tell he meant business. He had on a blue pinstripe suit. Plus, he'd slicked down his hair and waxed his mustache. He'd retired from Zenith in the 60s. He had hunched shoulders from the twenty years he'd spent bent over circuits with a solder gun.

The story I'd heard was that, decades before, Reynolds had made a serious play for Old Lady Skeleton, who'd apparently been quite the looker. There'd even been talk of marriage. But Old Lady Skeleton dumped Reynolds and took up with the man who became Old Man Skeleton. Still, he was a sore winner, and he never liked seeing his rival drooling around his woman.

After Reynolds got a few in him, he made his way down the bar and sat next to Almost Mrs. Reynolds. At first, everything was okay. He bought the Skeletons a drink, and they talked about how Zenith and the neighborhood were going to hell.

"Young ones got it too good," Reynolds said.

"Lazy," Old Man Skeleton said.

"Japs work like dogs."

"Can't compete."

"Too soft."

"Didn't help Zenith when they started hirin' shines and spicks. Lazy fuckers."

"Look who's talkin'!" Old Lady Skeleton burst in. "Most times, they couldn't find you half the shift. Wasn't for the union, you'd been canned."

Reynolds stood up like he was going to get into it with her.

"Shut up, shut up," Old Man Skeleton said to his wife.

"Yeah, let's all settle down," I said.

But the cops bought the trio sombreros. And when they downed their tequila shots, I knew it meant trouble. The old bastards did not do well with hard liquor. It made Reynolds' libido rumble. It made Old Man Skeleton just plain mean.

Reynolds ordered still more shots.

"Not a good idea," I said.

"My money's no good?" Reynolds said.

"Your money's fine," I said.

"Well pour, then," Old Man Skeleton said.

And, I did. And, sure as hell, Reynolds started with Old Lady Skeleton. He leaned over until their shoulders touched and heads were close.

"Let's forget the past and talk the future, darlin'," Reynolds said. "Come on home with me, and I'll press ya against the wall."

"Promise?" she said.

"Guaranteed, baby."

She smiled, he smiled, their hands brushed, and Reynolds told her more of the things he'd do to her when he got her against that wall. It went on like that until Old Man Skeleton couldn't take it anymore. He turned to his wife and shouted, "Whore!"

"That's no way for a gentleman to treat a lady," Reynolds said.

"How would you know?" Old Man Skeleton said. "Mind your business."

"She is my business."

"She's my wife."

"Don't hold that against her."

Old Man Skeleton brought his cigarette to his lips and then elbowed Reynolds in the face.

Reynolds got up from his stool slowly. He got into his best boxer's stance. A little stream of blood trickled from his nose. "Come on," he said.

"Go home," Old Man Skeleton said.

"Chicken shit."

Old Man Skeleton squashed his cigarette, stood, and put his fists up. Railroad Bob jumped up from his booth, got between the two and hollered, "All right! All right, already!" And somehow for a second I thought he was gonna stop it, but he just said "I want a clean fight."

"Shut up, Bob," Old Man Skeleton said.

So I figured I'd have to stop it myself. But then everybody started making bets. And I figured, how often do you see two eighty-year-olds in sombreros punch each other out? Within a minute, the whole bar had money riding on the fight, including me.

The two danced around each other for a bit. Or maybe that's stretching it: they stumbled around slowly. The wide brims of the sombreros made it hard to land a punch. But after a few swings, both hats were on the floor.

Reynolds was the first to connect, making a right eye swell up. But Old Man Skeleton was tougher than I thought. He got inside and threw a left-right-left combination. Anybody below sixty could have blocked it, but Reynolds couldn't, and one of the punches connected with his uppers.

His dentures flew out of his mouth. They landed on the floor and broke into two pieces. Reynolds was rocked back on his heels and had to be held up by a few of the cops.

Railroad Bob stepped between the fighters, examined Reynolds' condition, and declared a technical knockout. He raised Old Man Skeleton's hand in the air and hollered: "The winner and still octogenarian champion of the world!"

"Shut up, Bob," Old Man Skeleton said.

The winners cheered and collected their bets. The losers booed and said Reynolds was a pussy. Reynolds pulled away from the cops' grip, picked up his teeth and put the pieces in his pocket. He came up to the bar. To keep himself steady, he had to grip the arm rail.

"Old Style," he said.

"No teeth, no drinks," I told him.

"My money's no good?"

"You'll drool."

"Fuck you."

Reynolds fumbled with his coat, threw it on, buttoned it, and after great effort, slicked back his hair with his hands. He stumbled to the door, turned around, and as he wobbled there, he yelled, "I'm a lover, not a fighter!"

"Last words are for fools," Railroad Bob said.

Reynolds pulled the door open and staggered out into the falling snow.

Old Man Skeleton put his sombrero back on and sat down next to his wife.

"My hero," she said.

"Whore," he said.

"You married me."

"Don't remind me."

◇◇◇

By the end of the night, there were only a few drinkers left.

Old Man Skeleton called me over, summoning me with a bony hand.

"What?" I asked.

"Wanna a pistol," he said. "Nothin' heavy. Revolver."

"So go buy one."

"Can't. Got a record. Can ya get me one?"

"No."

"Why?"

"Cause if ya don't shoot yourself, you'll end up shootin' your old lady."

"I need it," he said. "You know how it's getting here."

I didn't know what to say. That's what it'd become. The old man had nothing. He lived on his pension and social security. He never had more than twenty bucks on him. Still, the poor old fucker thought he needed a pistol to walk the three blocks from the tavern to his house. And the way things were, he was probably right.

◇◇◇

When you live in Chicago, you'll put up with gangsters, robbers, murderers, arsonists, rapists, drunks, junkies, hookers, feral cats, rabid dogs, rats, cockroaches, criminal cops, and worse politicians, but one thing you will not stand for is snow keeping you from making money. If a mayor wants to keep his job, he better make sure the streets get cleared.

Despite all the fucking taxes and payoffs they gouged from us, the machine didn't have enough people and equipment to fight the blizzard. So they offered $15 an hour to freelancers. Damn good money.

A couple mornings after our party, there was a story on the TV news about this Indiana farmer who'd taken the bait. He'd driven his front loader into the city and, for sixteen hours a day, seven days straight, he'd been clearing streets and alleys. When he was done, he went to the city for his pay, but the city said they couldn't pay him on the spot. They promised to send him a check.

I guess Farmer was smart enough to know that it'd be a hell of a long time before he'd see his money, if he saw it all, because on his way back to Indiana, he'd lost it. In the middle of rush hour traffic, he'd started clearing the Dan Ryan Expressway of commuters. He rammed anything on wheels.

The cops were called, and when they got there, they started shooting at Farmer, which pissed him off even more. So, instead of just ramming cars, he started raising the shovel and crushing roofs like they were beer cans.

The cops kept shooting and Farmer kept crushing until, finally, one of the cops got lucky with a head shot. But Farmer's foot was still on the gas. The front loader slammed into the back of a hatchback, which exploded and killed two student nurses.

Still, I had to laugh. If he'd asked anybody from Chicago, they could have saved him the trip. They'd have told him to never, ever trust anybody, especially the city, and to always get his money up front.

I got up, switched off the TV, and went to bed. Cleared streets were bad for the tavern business.

The weather stayed cold, and that meant a low turnout for our next poker game. It was just Jerry, the Reverend, Brain, and me. But even without much of an audience, Jerry still couldn't hold back. He started telling us the story of how he got the PCP weed, the stuff that had messed up Dog Breath.

"There was these kids from Young," he said. "We watched for a couple of weeks. We waited in the alley across from the schoolyard. Where the dumpsters are. We could see them, but they couldn't see us. I was sittin' shotgun drinkin' a beer and the Reverend was readin' some book. It was pretty fuckin' cold, and the Reverend wanted to leave. He figured they weren't comin.' But I knew better. 'cause I know what it's like bein' sixteen with a six pack on a Friday night with no place to go. Church boy here doesn't have a goddamn clue."

"Drunk," the Reverend said.

"Jesus whore," Jerry said. "Anyway, finally, a group of 'em came down the street toward Young. They all had on these long army jackets, and each one of 'em had a big bulge around the gut. The blonde kid was leadin' the way. All of a sudden, he turned around and hollered, 'To build a fire, assholes.' Now I don't know what the hell he's talkin' about, but it cracked Reverend up."

"It's a Jack London story, dumbshit," the Reverend said.

"Anyway," Jerry said, "When they reached the dumpsters, the blonde kid opened his coat and pulled out a six pack of tall boys. He took one and put the rest behind the dumpster. The others did the same. So, we had enough to roust 'em, and I wanted to, but asshole said we should give it some time."

"You need to let them get comfortable. Otherwise, they see it comin'," the Reverend said.

"So we waited," Jerry said. "It didn't get too boring. One of 'em did little tricks. He put a lit cigarette on the back of his hand, flipped it up in the air and caught it right in his mouth. Anyway, we waited 'till they were done with their first beer, and the Reverend put it in drive and we were about to do it, but these two girls pulled up in a brand new red Mustang."

"Daddy's car," the Reverend said.

"Definitely," Jerry said. "They looked scared. The driver kept looking around while her friend got out and went up to the blonde kid. He handed her a bag and she handed him the cash."

"Daddy's cash," the Reverend said.

"So, we waited until the Mustang left. Then the Reverend stomped the gas and we ended up right in front of the dumpsters. These idiots didn't know what the hell to do. They just stood there shakin'. I told 'em,

'Run, you're fucked.' We lined 'em up against the dumpster and put the beer on top of it. We emptied their pockets and put that stuff on top too. There was the usual shit. Cigarettes, combs, cash, rollin' papers. And they were scared, man. They were breathin' heavy. The air was filled with steam. Finally, we got to the blonde kid. He was starin' at the wall like, if he tried hard enough, he'd melt into it. I put my light on him. 'Nervous?' I said.

"'No, sir,' he said.'"

"'Should be,' I said. The Reverend reached into Blondie's jacket pockets and pulled out a roll of cash and a bunch of dope. He piled it right in front of the kid. 'Nervous now?' I said."

"'Shit,' he said.'"

"I threw the dope and cash in the trunk, and I put the kid in the car. Then we told the other goofs about the calls we'd been gettin' about noise and fights, and that they were a pain in the ass and we got better things to do than babysit the little fuckers."

"So the Reverend said, 'Line up, penguins.' And they knew what was comin'. And they didn't want to, but when we told 'em it was that or jail, they sure as hell lined up. Then, one by one, we shook up a tallboy and poured it down their pants."

Jerry started laughing like it was the funniest fuckin' story that had ever been told. It was a sick demented laugh. The Reverend smirked a little. Brain and I just kind of looked at him.

"So the rest of them picked up their shit and started waddlin' down the street. Funny shit. It was cold already, it was so cold the beer was steamin' off their pants. And the Reverend yelled, 'To build a fire, motherfuckers!'"

Again Jerry laughed. Again we didn't.

"So we got back in the squad with the blonde kid, and he was shakin', but I told him to relax. I told him if he gives us his connection, he walks. So he told us it's this guy who hangs over by Commonwealth Liquors. And, when I asked the kid what he looks like, he let out this little laugh. He told us we can't miss him 'cause he always wears a green velvet suit with matching green platforms that got clear heals with plastic gold fish floatin' in 'em."

"Well, at first I thought the kid was bullshittin', but then I figured nobody's *that* good a liar. But, before we let him go, the Reverend asked the kid if he liked Jack London. He said, 'Yeah.' He was smilin' like he thought the Reverend and him were gonna be book buddies or somethin'. And..."

"And I told him 'Jack London was a racist motherfucker,'" the Reverend said, cutting Jerry off.

Jerry gave the Reverend a look. "Yeah. Racist motherfucker. And the kid's face dropped. It was like tellin' him there's no Santa. He..."

"He got all pale," the Reverend interrupted again. "Hell, I didn't think you people could get any whiter."

"Are you finished?" Jerry said to the Reverend, who said nothing. "So we cut him loose and went over to

Chicago Avenue and, sure as hell, there was this motherfucker, who had to be close to seven feet, in a green velvet suit and green platforms standin' in front of Commonwealth Liquors. Christ, it was like he was wearin' a sign sayin': *Bust me*. So we got him into the squad and told him what he'd owe and when we'd pick it up. Then the Reverend..."

"I told him to..." the Reverend started.

But Jerry pounded the table with his fist. Chip towers toppled. "Can I finish a fuckin' story?" he asked.

The Reverend shrugged, and Jerry shook his head and muttered something that sounded like: *dumb fucking nigger*.

The Reverend's eyes narrowed, like: *We'll just see about that*. And Brain and I gave both of them a look like, OK, whatever.

"After that, I told him to lose the suit and platforms, 'cause even we couldn't keep his ass outta jail in that getup." And Jerry leaned back like this was the greatest story ever, like it was God's gift to stories.

I figured it was time to cash in. But Jerry was my ride home, so I knew I had to wait. He hadn't lost enough.

I'd known cops all my life. They got paid shit money for a shit job. If they took a couple of bucks on the side to feed their family and pay a few bills, I had no problem with that. Hell, they were just doing what everybody does. But all the money Jerry took was for women, gambling, and to pay off juice loans. He was always putting Fatboy down, but he was just like any drunk or dope fiend. Money was for feeding his habit.

When he was gambling, he was blind to everything else.

Most of the time, I kept my mouth shut about it, but that night, I didn't. Maybe it was because, with every passing day, I had less to lose. Or maybe I was sick of Jerry's stories. Or maybe I was just sick of Jerry. But anyway I said: "Why fuck with kids?"

He gave me a look like he didn't know who I was. "Come on! It was funny."

"Wasn't funny when the cops fucked with us."

"We lived."

"Chicago's finest messin' with kids with no place to go. Tough guys. When you're through losin', I'll be upstairs."

I headed up outta the basement and had a beer at the bar. But my mind was still downstairs. I couldn't help but think that I was stuck, that the currency exchange was coming up, and it was gonna have to happen, and it woulda been fine, except I was stuck, and this is who I was stuck with, and it wasn't gonna end well.

By the time he was done, Jerry had borrowed another hundred from Brain. When we got to the car, I had to give him money for gas.

Whistling

Western Electric workers were paid every other Friday. We chose a Thursday a couple weeks after the blizzard. The streets and alleys were mostly clear, but it was bitter cold.

The Reverend made sure that we got a paddy wagon. He parked it in the garage. After I closed, Fatboy and I climbed in to the back.

Fatboy and I sat on the cold metal bench. The smell of the piss and vomit of drunks laid on us like a blanket. I watched as the street lights flickered through the metal mesh of the back window. At our feet was a duffel bag with everything we needed.

Even though my life wasn't worth much, I kept thinking that letting Jerry in on the score was a mistake. I kept thinking that the only thing he'd ever really been good at lately was fucking up. My heart pounded and I took quick breaths. I tried to calm down by counting the lights as they went by.

Fatboy asked me if I was okay.

"Yeah," I said.

"It's gonna work out," he said. "Do how we practiced."

The Reverend backed the wagon into place. We could hear the squawk of the police radio. I couldn't help but think about what Jerry had called him, back at the poker game, and I couldn't help but thinking he was going to have his revenge somehow, on Jerry, on all of us. My hands were shaking a bit. It was hard to tcll if it was from the fear or the Huntington's.

"Unless you're crazy like Jerry, you never get used to it," Fatboy said. "I'm always scared. But then, when it starts, it goes. The job's all I think about."

Jerry got out of the cab, walked back, and told us we could start. We climbed out into the dark and cold.

Fatboy took a blowtorch from the bag and started burning big squares into the door. I stood by and used a fire extinguisher to spray foam on flames. At one point, the tremors kicked in. I lost control and I dropped the extinguisher. The fucking thing banged onto the concrete, loud as hell in the dark quiet alley.

"Be careful," Fatboy hissed.

I rubbed my fingers. "Cramped up," I said.

We went through two torches. Then just as we started prying the wood from the door, Jerry banged on the side of the wagon. An old man was pushing a cart full of cans through the alley. He stopped and started walking toward the wagon. The Reverend got out.

"I'm a natural born man and do not fear you," the old man said.

"Get lost," The Reverend said. That sent the old guy on his way. When he was out of sight, we broke down the rest of the door.

We cleared the wood away. Fatboy was right. There were two steel bars. He grabbed a pair of bolt cutters, but the bars weren't padlocked. They were held in by pins. All he had to do was pull the pins and push. We piled the wood, torches and the extinguisher next to the door.

I tapped on the side of the wagon. Jerry jumped out, turned on a flashlight and led us in. I followed with the refrigerator dolly.

At the end of a long hallway was the currency exchange office. The safe was old and black and had faded lettering. It stood on four legs with just enough room for me to slip the dolly under it.

Meanwhile Jerry had wandered up front. He jammed a screwdriver into the cashier drawers and pried them open.

"What the fuck you doin'?" I said.

"Tokens," he said.

"What?"

"Bus tokens."

And even though he hadn't taken the bus since high school, we had to wait until the idiot stuffed his pockets until they bulged.

"Crazy motherfucker," the Reverend said. And again I thought about what Jerry had said at the poker game.

I slid the dolly in place. Jerry started singing "Whistle While You Work."

"Shut up," the Reverend said.

"What?" Jerry said. "We're elves. Get it?"

"Dwarves," the Reverend said.

"Huh?"

"It's from *Snow White and the Seven Dwarves*."

"So what?"

"Elves are make believe. Dwarves are real people, just small."

"Fuck it," Jerry said. "I'm a elf."

"Jesus Christ," I said. "Less whistle, more work."

Jerry put the dolly straps on and pulled them tight. Then the Reverend and Jerry pushed while Fatboy and I pulled. As we rolled backwards down the hallway, it was so heavy we had to put our bodies in front of the thing. Even though Jerry shined the flashlight, we couldn't see a thing. About halfway, Fatboy almost tripped.

"Careful, Dopey," Jerry said.

"Okay, Piggy," Fatboy said.

"Piggy isn't one of 'em," I said.

"He is now," the Reverend smirked.

"Hey!" Jerry exclaimed. "You know what PIG stands for? Pride, integrity, and guts."

The Reverend laughed and said, "Well, you got the guts part."

We finally got the thing out of the doorway and wrestled the dolly down the icy alley and over to the paddywagon. When we lifted and shoved the thing up into the back, Jerry's face got so red I thought he was going to blow an artery.

Fatboy and I climbed in and Jerry locked the doors. We just sat there in the cold for a couple minutes, and finally I heard him get in the front with the Reverend.

As we rode back, my arm suddenly decided to wander. It looked like a cobra rising out of a basket. It made a few waves in front of my face before it settled back down at my side. Fatboy stared at it.

"Arm cramped," I said. "Stretchin' it."

"Get a lotta cramps," he said.

"Gettin' old."

Street lights strobed, wagon rocked, heart slowed, muscles loosened, and I slumped against the wall of the wagon and thought about how getting old was a luxury I'd never know.

◇◇◇

We unloaded the safe in the garage. Behind it, there was a table with drills, drill bits, Italian Christmas tree lights, extra-long Phillips and flathead screwdrivers, chalk, a measuring tape, a flashlight, and a very, very thin telescope.

Jerry stayed to keep an eye on us, and the Reverend went to park the paddywagon around the corner. I felt anxious when he left, thinking about what else he might be up to. But I couldn't keep thinking about it. We weren't done, not by a long shot.

There are different ways to open a safe. You can blow the hell out of it, fuck with the combination, or drill. Since I wanted my building in one piece, and Fatboy didn't have a lot of experience with safes, we drilled.

First, Fatboy measured a spot from the side of the safe to the middle of the dial. He made a matching mark on the back. To cover the noise, we switched on a big floor fan.

He drilled for a while, and then it was my turn. Somewhere in there the Reverend had come back, and I was a little relieved, but he and Jerry just stood there and watched us like they were done working for the night, and I didn't much like that. I kneeled on one knee and put my weight behind the drill, after a few minutes, the vibration made my arms go numb. I had to stop and shake them until I felt the blood flow back into my hands.

After a few tries, the drill was so hot I had to put on work gloves. It burned itself out before the bit became dull. We switched it out and Fatboy took another turn.

We went through two drills before the steel gave way. Fatboy fed the Christmas tree lights through the hole and plugged them in. When we switched off the overhead, we could see a small ray of light coming from inside the safe.

We kept drilling until the thing was dotted with holes. Fatboy tried to pick up the telescope, but dropped it. His hands were cramping, too, and he had to massage them until they'd let him work.

I plugged in the Christmas tree lights again. Fatboy knelt down, slipped the telescope through one of the holes, and took a look. He smiled and handed it to me.

I could see cash. A lot of cash.

Almost as important, I could see the screws for the plate that held the dial. Fatboy grabbed a screwdriver and put it through a few of the holes until he found the right one. He tried to turn the screw, but he had to let go of the telescope and use both hands. After a few tries, he finally loosened it. They were all tough, but it was a rush every time we heard one drop to the floor of the safe. After the last one dropped, I grabbed the dial, pulled, and the whole thing gave way.

I turned the handle and pulled. When the door swung open, we saw more money than either of us had ever seen. The thing was stuffed with bundles of hundreds, twenties, tens, fives, and ones. There were bags of rolled quarters, dimes, nickels, and pennies. The sight of it made me step back. Jerry and the Reverend were grinning, standing there like best buddies. Fatboy fell to his knees, put his hands on top of his head, and smiled. "Holy shit," he said. "Holy shit."

◇◇◇

Fatboy, The Reverend, Jerry, and I sat in the basement and counted the money. It took hours, but when we were done, the total was over $150,000.

My cut was much more than I needed. At first, I thought of all it could mean. I had visions of selling the tavern and renting a small apartment, a place that no one would know about except for Rita and me. I fantasized about going to a lawyer and setting up a fund, money just for her, money that Jerry could never get his hands on. And, when it was time, I would find a private hospital where some blonde twenty-year-old nurse would feed me and give me sponge baths. It might not be half bad, I figured. She could push me around in my cushioned wheelchair, and maybe they'd have a patio and a green garden, and she could take me out there, and eventually I'd be out there in the sunlight and I would take my last breath. Come to think of it, it would've been one hell of a death.

Meanwhile, Fatboy and Jerry were going on and on about what they were going to do with their take. Jerry said he was going to buy a cabin in Wisconsin. Fatboy said he knew a perfect bar for sale in Lincoln Park. But the Reverend didn't say anything. He just stared at the stacks of wrapped bills piled on the table.

I was surprised that he saw it before me, but that's when it hit me: What was a currency exchange doing with that much cash?

"Too much," I said.

"What?" Fatboy said.

"Money," I said.

"Relax," Jerry said.

"Nobody keeps that much cash unless they're hidin' it," I said.

"Dope money," the Reverend said.

"Even better," Jerry said. "They won't call the cops."

"Shit," the Reverend said. "They'll come lookin' for it."

"They don't know us," Jerry said.

"Can't spend it," the Reverend said. "Not for a long time."

"Paranoid fuckers," Jerry said.

But the Reverend was right. "If we start throwing cash around, how long do ya think it'll be before somebody finds out? If it's not the ones we ripped off, it'll be the government," I said.

It took some time, but finally even Jerry agreed that the smartest thing to do was not spend the money for at least a year and, even then, not on anything big. We agreed there'd be no more scores, and we'd keep a low profile.

The Reverend and I divided up the cash and put the shares in shopping bags. When I handed Jerry his, I said, "Don't spend it."

He said he wasn't stupid. Then, like a kid at Halloween, he took a quick peek into the bag and smiled.

"Shit," the Reverend said. He snatched up his share and trotted up the stairs. Jerry followed him, singing "Whistle While You Work."

"Shut the fuck up," the Reverend said.

"What? I'm a elf," Jerry said.

When they were gone, Fatboy turned to me. "I don't wanna carry this home alone. Not in this neighborhood."

"I'll keep it here for you."

He gave me a look, all suspicious like. "I'll take it. Just...gimme one of the .38s."

And all of a sudden, I got nervous about him ripping me off, screwing me over. "Don't worry about it," I told him. "I'll keep it separate from mine."

I grabbed the bag. He let go reluctantly.

I took a chair over to the side of the basement and wedged it up into a little cubbyhole under the floor joists. "See? There you go."

Still, he was giving me this look which I didn't much like. And it occurred to me maybe he was going to come back, spend it all buying that bar, call attention to the whole thing. Maybe he was the one I needed to worry about.

And even apart from that, the way I'd hid the money had disturbed the cement dust up around the cubbyhole. If someone came down here, like Jerry or the Reverend, they'd see right away that somebody'd been over there. Now that I noticed it, I couldn't stop noticing it.

I grabbed a case of potato chips, handed it to him, and told him to take it upstairs and stock the rack. He gave me a look like: *Now?* But I just glared at him.

I waited until he was upstairs. When I heard the basement door shut, I moved his money, and mine, over to the coal chute.

Bizarre Currency Exchange Burglary

by James Thompson

A West Side currency exchange was raided in a bold burglary early Friday morning. James Caruso, owner of the Island Currency Exchange at 5900 W. Roosevelt Road, says he arrived at the start of the workday to find that someone had broken in by burning down the back door. When he entered the business, he discovered that the safe had been taken. He estimated it contained approximately $20,000.

The police have no suspects.

Skippin' Welk

Saturday morning I finally had a chance to see Rita.

Jerry was working, and she'd sent the kids to the neighbor's, and we had the place to ourselves. She was lying next to me with her head resting on my shoulder and her hand on my chest.

On the wall at the foot of her bed, there was a painting of a woman walking down an alley. The old lady was pushing a cart of bricks through snow. Her knees were bent and her shoulders hunched. She wore a long overcoat with a hood that hid her face. She was barefoot.

"What's it mean?" I asked.

"Whatever you think it means."

"Tough times."

"That's what it means."

We listened to the noises outside, landlords scraping ice from the sidewalks and shoveling salt, boots crunching it underfoot. We stayed quiet for a long time until finally she said, "After your parents died, do you remember calling me?"

I said that all I remembered back then was the pizza guy's number, and how to get another bottle, but it was a lie. I didn't remember much of what I'd said, but I did remember.

When I knew Jerry was working, I'd get a few in me and dial her number. Then the next morning, I'd wake up with the phone next to me, and I wouldn't remember what I'd said, but I'd know who I'd called. My stomach would tighten up. I'd swear to myself I wouldn't drink that much again, but the shame would mix with the grief and fear, and the weight of it would be too much for me. By the time night rolled around, I'd be drunk and reaching for the phone yet again.

"It was always the same," she said. "At first, you'd be sweet. You'd tell me I was beautiful, and that you loved me and wanted me to be happy. But then I'd hear your voice change. You'd call me a bitch, or worse, like it was me that left you. You'd start cryin' and beggin' me to help you. I'd have to tell you over and over that it was going to be alright, until finally you'd pass out. I used to lay there and listen to you breathe."

"Shoulda hung up," I said.

"I liked it. It was like you were sleeping next to me. I had you to myself."

"I'm glad those times are over. I'm glad it's all over. I thought Jerry was gonna fuck it up, but he didn't. We've got money now."

"Jerry. Jerry is still..." Her voice trailed off.

I wanted to know what she was thinking, but I didn't want to ask. "I still can't hate him. As much as I want to. If he hadn't saved the bar, I'd probably be dead or in the street."

"I had to push him," she said.

"What?"

"He doesn't do things like that on his own."

I never asked Jerry why he'd done it. I was just glad he did it. But, when she told me, it made sense. "Christ," I said. "Am I that stupid?"

She took my face in her hands and kissed me. "Don't worry," she said. "Lots of people can't see what's right in front of them."

Then we watched as my arm lifted and lowered itself in front of me. Then a tremor shot through my body and she held me until it passed.

◇◇◇

I was working again that night. It wasn't busy. Fatboy and I stood at the end of the bar smoking cigarettes. There were a few Zeniths and cops.

The Skeletons and Railroad Bob were arguing about what to watch on TV. On Saturdays, Old Man Skeleton always watched Lawrence Welk. I even turned off the jukebox for him. It killed me to listen to that shit. Still, I gave the old man his one hour a week. But Railroad Bob was a Jane Goodall freak and said he wanted to watch a National Geographic Special on chimps.

"I'm not skippin' Welk for a buncha fuckin' monkeys," Old Man Skeleton said.

"They aint monkeys. They're our cousins," Railroad Bob said.

"Not missin' Welk."

"Lawrence Welk is the gonorrhea of American music."

"Well at least he aint a goddamn monkey."

I knew that Bob would keep whining if we didn't put on the monkey show. So, I told Old Man Skeleton that, for once, we'd skip Welk. He got really pissed. He gulped down his beer, stood up, put on his coat, and told Old Lady Skeleton to do the same.

"I aint leavin'," she said. "I like monkeys."

Old Man Skeleton stomped toward the door. Railroad Bob shouted after him, "Don't go. Patience is bitter, but its fruit is sweet."

"Go fuck yourself," Old Man Skeleton said, and walked out.

We were halfway into the monkey show when we heard the sirens. I could see red flashing lights through the glass blocks, off in the distance but coming our way. My heart pounded. For a second, I thought they were for me. But then they rumbled on by: fire trucks.

Usually, one of us would have run out too see what was going on, but it was cold and the show was pretty good. So we didn't know until a few minutes later, when Mongo came in.

Mongo was big, with red frizzy hair, and a beard to match. I'd banned him, but I still let him buy six packs. He was just wearing a t-shirt and jeans, but I didn't think much of it because Mongo was a crazy bastard. (He got his nickname for slapping a police horse after a rock concert. What's more, when the cop was dragging him off to the paddy wagon, Mongo kept hollering, going on and on about how the horse had started it, and it was all self-defense.) I grabbed a six pack, gave it to him, and took his cash to ring up the sale. And he just turned and walked out without a word. But through the glass block I saw him stop, open a can, and guzzle it down.

We still hadn't gotten rid of the safe. I didn't want to draw attention to the place. There'd already been noise complaints. I didn't want another one for letting a bloated redheaded maniac drink in front of my place. I went outside to tell him to move along. That's when I saw the smoke.

A couple of blocks away, an apartment building was on fire. Flames and smoke were pouring out of the windows. The fire truck was parked in the middle of North Avenue. A couple of firemen were on top of the building cutting holes into the roof. A few more were aiming hoses at the building. The water mixed with snow. A grey slush covered the street. Mongo didn't look at me. He just kept looking at the fire and drinking.

"All my shit," he said. "Gone."

"Come in," I said.

"Banned," he said.

"Fuck it," I said.

I opened the door for him. He came inside. I sat him down in a booth. I got a coat from the garage and gave it to him. I told him he could sleep in the booth that night, but tomorrow he'd have to find someplace else. I gave him a hundred bucks and told Fatboy that Mongo could have as many draft beers as he could hold. I tried to go back to watching the monkey show.

People with money are always going on about poor people spending their money on cigarettes, dope, and booze, but they just don't get it. Mongo spent his last few bucks on a six pack because it didn't matter. In the morning, he'd still be a poor, crazy son of a bitch with nothing. What the hell difference would five bucks make?

"What was that about?" one of the cops asked.

"Fuckin' fire outside. Apartment building."

He shook his head. "Jesus. There goes the neighborhood, huh? Fuckin' animals. Who burns a place down? As if it isn't bad enough, with all the crime..."

"Yeah," I said. "Fuckin' criminals."

The phone rang: Jerry.

"Where the fuck you been?" he asked. He was agitated.

"Home, then here. Where the fuck else would I be? Did you hear about the..."

"I was callin' your fuckin' place all morning," he cut me off. "Tryin' to get ahold of you."

I thought about being with Rita. I took a deep breath. "Why, what's up?"

"The Reverend. He's gone."

Dope Makes You Sloppy

We met just over the bridge at Hanson Park Stadium. Jerry, Fatboy, and I sat on the wooden benches, blowing into our fists, stomping our feet, and passing a pint of Jack between us.

"Gone," Jerry said. "Never showed up."

"Don't mean he's gonna give us up," I said.

"Don't mean he isn't," Fatboy said.

"So what happened?" I asked.

"It was our first shift together since the currency exchange. No call, no show. That's not like the Reverend. So I called him: no answer. I called again and again before I went out: nothing. So I got in the cruiser, went by his building. He didn't answer his door. I watched the building for hours. No sign of him."

"Did ya go in?" Fatboy asked.

"No sign of him," Jerry repeated.

I said the best thing to do was to think the worst. We agreed to get rid of any stuff left from the burglaries and never to meet in the tavern.

Then we passed the bottle between us until it was gone. Jerry took the empty and made a sidearm throw. It skipped over the snow-covered AstroTurf until it skidded to a stop. Then, suddenly, Jerry looked tired. His shoulders slumped and he tilted his head to one side as if it was just too heavy to keep upright.

"Seven years," he said. "And this is what he does."

"You don't know," I said. "Maybe somethin' happened to him."

"Nothin' happens to the Reverend. He took his piece and disappeared. Left town. How the fuck do you think that makes me look, that he just disappeared?" Then he sighed. "Fuck it. Wanna go to Cicero?"

"Why?"

"Get a drink."

"What's wrong with the bars around here?"

"Gotta pay a guy."

"With what money?"

"My money, asshole. Don't worry about the new stuff. I ain't touchin' it."

But the way he said it, I knew he was lying and that, no matter what promises he made, he'd dip into the money. Instead of playing cards once a week, he'd make it an everyday thing. On his days off, he'd go out to Maywood and bet heavy on the trotters. When he wasn't doing that, he'd lay bets with bookies.

I figured maybe he was right and the Reverend was in the process of screwing us over. But then again, he might have just thought his partner was a degenerate gambler who couldn't be trusted to keep his promises. If that was the case, the Reverend had made the smart move. He took his cut and left, so he wouldn't get caught holding the bag. That's when I realized he was smarter than all of us.

If I could've, I'd have done the same thing. If I'd been smart, right then, I'd have grabbed my money and took off. Jerry didn't give a shit about me. He went out of his way to fuck me over. I owed him nothing.

But I couldn't. I had to see about Rita.

Fatboy and I headed for the Central Avenue Bridge. It was cold, but the whiskey in my belly kept me warm. Fatboy was wearing his thin jean jacket with just a sweatshirt underneath. Every once in a while, his teeth would chatter and he'd shiver.

He didn't say anything until we started across the bridge. "Not going back to prison," he said.

"Even if the Reverend is gonna give us up, we might get off. This is America. With enough money, you can buy your way out of anything," I said.

He gave me a look like: Yeah, right.

"You know why you went to prison?" I asked.

"Dope made me sloppy."

"Dope made you poor. The Outfit's killed truckloads and not one has gone to prison for it. They aint geniuses. They got money. They're connected."

We walked on for a bit. I said I wasn't worried that much about getting caught, and I even kind of believed it. But I was worried about what Rita would say when she found out. "Gonna tell your sister about the Reverend?"

"Rather go to prison."

"She's not stupid. She's gonna find out."

He looked at me like a kid who'd just broken a neighbor's window. "Will you tell her?"

"Yeah."

When we got to the top of the bridge, a train rumbled beneath and blasted us with a wave of snow. We shoved our hands in our pockets, hunched our shoulders, and started walking faster. When it was gone, he pulled the sleeve of my coat and we stopped.

"What? It's cold," I said.

"What are you doing with my sister, anyway?"

"Not sure."

"Where's it goin'?"

"Don't know."

"Well when will you fuckin' know?" It was the first time I'd seen him get really angry. "Look, I love my sister. Jerry's an asshole, but he's stuck around."

"So far." I smirked.

"You gonna stick around? You gonna take care of somebody else's kids?"

I told him I loved her.

He looked away from me. I knew he didn't believe me, and I couldn't blame him. I was a thief, a liar, and a hustler. Why wouldn't I hustle his sister too? So, I convinced him the only way I knew how. I told him the truth.

I told him that the problems with my arms and hands weren't because they went numb or because I was getting older. "I got Huntington's," I said. "Won't be sticking around for anybody."

"Rita know?"

"That's why we're together," I said. "I love your sister. Whatever I can do for her, I'll do."

We started walking again. And then, maybe it was because somebody'd finally thought enough of him to tell him the truth, or maybe it was the whiskey, or maybe it was just because he couldn't handle the weight of his own secret anymore, but, whatever the reason, he told me about Mr. Krause.

He said that he was so strung out that, most of the time, he didn't know what he was doing. All the burglaries melted together into a haze. "All I thought about was dope and money," he said. "I was so fucked up I stole Rita's stereo and tried to sell it back to her."

The day he'd done it was a typical day of hustling for him. When he passed Mr. Krause's house, he took a quick look around. All the windows and doors were closed, and a couple of newspapers were on the front porch.

"I should've checked better, but when you're dope sick, you get careless," he said. "I broke a basement window with a hammer and climbed in. I went up the basement steps and opened the door. The old man was sitting at the kitchen table eating a sandwich. He looked at me like me being there was no big deal. It was like he was expecting me. He said, 'Hi, Jimmy.' So, I said, 'Hi, Mr. Krause.' I asked him if he had any money. He said he didn't. I pulled him up to his feet. That's when he got scared. I pushed him through the house. He kept asking, 'Why are you doing this?' I didn't answer. I just kept pushing. We went through the whole place. I ripped it apart. But he hadn't been lying. There was no money. It meant I'd have to keep hustling and it pissed me off. This rage came and I lost it. I hit him with the hammer until he fell. I grabbed what I could and left."

"I don't even remember who I sold his shit to," Fatboy went on. "The next thing I remember was you and Jerry dragging me out of the dope house."

I took a deep breath. Cold air stabbed my chest. "Of all the people," I said. "All the people in the neighborhood."

He shrugged.

Fatboy's mother Deirdre had the personality of a granite slab.

In Ireland, when she was twelve, her mother had given her to the nuns. They'd brought her to Texas, where she did six years hard labor. One day, they handed her a suitcase, told her she didn't have *the calling,* and shoved her onto a Chicago-bound train. She married at eighteen and gave birth six months later.

I never saw a smile on the woman's face. Hell, I never saw any expression on her face at all. She treated her kids like shit. Anytime she left the house, she locked them out. She'd leave them on the streets for hours. If they were hungry or had to use the bathroom, they had to ask the goddamn neighbors.

Rita told me that she and Fatboy had started ripping off stores because they couldn't stand the pity of the neighbors. Every time anyone gave them something to eat, they'd shake their heads, *tsk...tsk...tsk,* and whisper to each other. When she'd told me about all that, I thought: Jesus Christ, they were just kids. Why can't people give something to somebody without making them feel like shit about it?

But Mr. and Mrs. Krause had been different. Mr. Krause was a golf nut. He'd landscaped his yard into a putting green. When he was young, they said he was good enough to be a pro. One story spread around the neighborhood was that, when he was in high school, he was challenged to a round by Machine Gun Jack McGurn, the guy behind the St. Valentine's Day Massacre. When they played, as they strolled down the fairway, they were flanked by gangsters with machine guns. Mr. Krause wanted to stay healthy. He let McGurn win.

When Fatboy was little, Mr. Krause used to bring him into their backyard. He had a half dozen golf balls and clubs, and they'd spend an hour trying to sink putts into plastic cups. Mrs. Krause had a garage stuffed with paints, brushes, canvases, plaster, hammers, and chisels. She'd bring Rita out there and give her art lessons.

The Krauses always fed them. Rita used to tell me their house was like a TV house: red vinyl kitchen chairs, a red formica table, a bowl of plastic fruit, and rooster cookie jar. The Krauses gave them sandwiches on real plates, and always watched them eat, but Rita said it didn't feel like pity. They really seemed to like Fatboy and her. They really seemed to care.

But after a while, Rita and Fatboy stopped going to see the Krauses. Rita said it was better to face the world as it was, than to get attached to something that could never be. It was better to get used to taking care of yourself. Better to bite the hand.

After all Fatboy told me about Mr. Krause, I just nodded and tried not to look surprised. Even though I'd helped with his alibi, I'd always had had a hard time believing that he'd really done it.

We were almost over the bridge when Fatboy asked me not to tell anybody, ever. I said I wouldn't. "We all got ghosts," I said.

The wind was at our backs and shoved us forward. In front of us, snow blew from roofs, and smoke puffed from chimneys.

I asked him not to tell anybody about the Huntington's. "Nobody drinks at a dead guy's bar," I said.

◇◇◇

We sat around the table drinking beer and bluffing each other. Besides Jerry and me, there were two old cops, and of course Brain, who sat with a box of chips and stack of ashtrays next to him. He had his sleeves rolled up, and he dealt quickly. His wrist snapped and cards spun.

One of the old guys wouldn't shut up about the Cubs. "They're shit," he said. "Haven't had a real shot since Durocher in '69. Shoulda traded Banks. Let's play two, my ass. Fucker could barely play one. He put asses in the seats. That's all Wrigley gave a fuck about. Right? Gum hustling motherfucker wouldn't know a baseball if it hit him in the nuts. Faggot."

It was funny at first, but he kept going on and on about Wrigley and how the real reason they didn't play night ball was because the cheap cocksucker wouldn't put in lights. "That's why they'll never make it to a goddamn World Series," he said.

We listened to the old man babble for a few more hands, and then Brain slipped in some gossip. "Heard about the burglary?" he said.

"What burglary?" I said.

"Currency exchange on Roosevelt," he said, "Heard it was a Outfit bank. Paper said they got twenty. Heard it was a lot more."

"Huh." Fear kicked in the Huntington's. My hands start to shake.

I got up and went to the men's room. I stayed there until I calmed myself down. I told myself again that I just needed enough time to get rid of the tavern and the license. And to talk to Rita.

When I came out, I saw Brain slipping Jerry a wad of cash.

I knew I was going to die, but I wanted to be the one to choose the place and how it happened. Otherwise, what good was the risk I'd been taking? So I waited until after the game to talk to Jerry about it. We sat at the bar.

"What if it's true?" I said. "What if it is an Outfit place?"

"They don't know it was us," he said.

"Keep doin' what you're doin' and they will. Why you borrowin'?"

"I'm not."

"I fuckin' saw it."

Then the fucker actually smiled. With everything he did, he was like a teenager with a girl in the backseat and no rubber. He didn't think about how any of it would turn out. "I needed it."

"You lost it already?"

"Some. I invested most of it."

"Invested it?" I almost burst a blood vessel. "In what?"

"Dry cleaners."

"What the fuck do you know about the dry cleaning business?"

"I don't. Tram does."

Here I really almost lost it. The only thing that kept me from losing it was the thought of who mighta been listening. "Who the fuck is Tram?"

Jerry laughed a little and started talking.

It turned out Tram was a stripper he had on the side. He'd met her two years before at a Cicero afterhours place. They'd shot pool and had a few drinks. "I thought she'd be like the others," he said. "But we hit it off. She's so smart. She came over here with nothin'. No family. No friends. Couldn't even speak the fucking language. Smart, though! She got to Chicago and worked cleaning hotel rooms for a bit, but she found out taking her clothes off and hustling drinks paid a lot better. But she's doin' it right. She saved her money and bought a condo. She learned English and saved some more. And now she's taking business classes. Business classes, Andy!"

I could hear pride in every word. He admired her. I'd never heard him talk about Rita like that, even when they'd first started dating. But I couldn't take it any more. "Rita's beautiful and smart, asshole."

Here his eyes narrowed, like he was wondering why I cared. "Rita always wants somethin'."

"All a stripper wants is your money." As soon as I said it, I knew I shouldn't have.

He leaned toward me and pointed a finger. "Tram didn't ask me for shit," he said. "She was gonna hustle until she had enough. I tried to give it to her, but she wouldn't take it unless it was a loan. We got a contract."

"You signed a contract?" I said.

He grinned like it was the smartest fuckin' thing he'd ever done. "Yeah!"

"A contract with a stripper."

He gave me a look like he was gonna hit me. But he just said: "She's different. She didn't ask me for shit." Like a broken fucking record.

I shook my head. "If somebody asks...or should I say, *when* somebody asks, how you gonna explain where you got the money?"

He burst out laughing. "You worry too much!"

Again I just shook my head. I was starting to realize how much I truly envied the Reverend. He could get away, but I was chained to Jerry. For years, I'd carried him with every step I took. Other people might look back on their childhood friends and think of baseball games, school dances, or maybe a schoolyard fight or two. But when I looked at Jerry, I remembered a kid who kept me from getting burned. I saw somebody who, even though he hated his junkie brother-in-law, loved his wife enough to drag him out of a dope house and give him a trumped up alibi. And even though Rita had put him up to it, when I was a drunk, he'd saved me from the street. How do you walk away from somebody like that?

Still, I wanted to shove his face into the bar. Loyalty fucks up everything.

The Thing Shatters

It was a work day for Rita, at Zenith. I watched the jeans slide over her hips, the tank top fold down over her breasts, the brush push through her hair. And I laid in her bed and thought about all the time I'd thrown away, time I could have spent looking at her.

"It's a shame," I said as she put on her long-sleeved flannel.

"What is?"

"Covering up your body."

She smiled, just a little. "Got no choice. It's hot as hell on the floor, but it's better than getting cut. The tubes run on a conveyer above us. They try to keep the roof patched, but sometimes there's a leak. It only takes a drop or two. The tubes are so hot that, when water hits one, the thing shatters. Sometimes, there's a chain reaction and two or three explode. I never look up. Once, I saw a girl get it in the face. I put my head down and cover it with my hands. Thousands of little pieces of glass rain down. Covers everything."

"You ever get cut?"

She rolled her eyes. "We all have. But there's worse to worry about. They give us memos telling us that some chemical's been banned 'cause it causes cancer. Most of the time, we've been using it forever. There's always stories of people dying a year or two after they retire."

"Well...be careful, OK."

She shook her head. "Are you bein' careful?"

"How do you mean?"

"Everything you've been doin'?" She poked me in the chest.

I sat up and grabbed my shirt so I could get the hell outta there. "What we've been doin' was your idea!"

"Well, think about who you're doin' it with, and who you're doin' it to."

And that was when I wondered if she knew about the Reverend. Or if Jerry'd told her about the currency exchange maybe bein' an Outfit bank. Still, I wanted to set her mind at ease. "We're fine."

Her face got tight. Her lips curled and her eyes narrowed. It was a look I'd seen before, a look she gave Jerry all the time. "Really?"

"Really."

"Just...keep an eye out. I'm workin' a straight job. I've only got one person to worry about." She threw on her coat, leaned over, kissed me, and said good bye.

I waited until I heard the front door close before putting on my clothes. I went out the back, slipped through the backyard and into the icy alley. As I walked back to the bar, my mind was a mush of Jerry and the Reverend and the Outfit and Rita, and the glass cutting into her, and how much she needed to get out.

The cold was a razor. It found skin and cut. Before going outside for anything, I had to decide if it was worth the pain. It was a Monday morning and I was sick of cereal. I decided sliders from White Castle was worth it. I put on my coat, kept my head down, and fought my way down the block.

When I got to North and Central, all the traffic lights were frozen green. Before I could cross the street, a car slammed into another. The two drivers got out, screamed at each other, and started throwing punches.

That's when I saw him. He was standing at the bus stop. He was tall and thin and wore a Brach's jacket over a hooded sweatshirt. He had a wool cap pulled around his ears. He had on gloves. In one hand was a paperback. He was watching the fight too. I thought about Gacy and the list of names, and how he hadn't been on it. I called his name, but he didn't answer.

When I got closer, I saw that he was too old.

Hope can shove what's real out of the way. I wanted it to be him because I wanted to be the one to have found Mrs. Connolly's son. I wanted to be the one to tell her. I wanted to be the reason she stopped searching, the reason she started sleeping through the night. I wanted to do just one goddamn thing that was right.

North and Central

◇◇◇

In the wee early hours of the next Sunday morning, after the cops and Zeniths had gone, I was doing the books.

Fatboy was with me. He'd gotten it into his head that he was going to use his share to open a leather bar on the North Side. I didn't know what that was, but I was pretty sure it had something to do with queers. I told him that, with his record, he couldn't get a license to cut hair, let alone own a bar, but he said he was going to get somebody to front for him.

For once, I pushed away all my streetwise bullshit. I found myself hoping everything would work out for him and he'd get what he wanted.

"You trust this guy?" I asked.

"Yeah."

"Good. That's all that matters. Trust."

I turned back to the books, all spread out on the table. I needed to add up the take, but he kept interrupting me. Finally, I gave up and stopped counting.

"You gonna let me do this?" I asked at last.

"Sorry, it's just...I got so many questions."

I took a deep breath. "All right. What's your biggest one?"

"How do you make it look legit?"

"Keep it simple. First pay the people who really fuck with you. You can stall everybody else. They might hassle you, but you don't want to piss off the IRS or the cops."

"How much should I skim?"

I could have given the answer, but, sooner or later, he'd be on his own and there'd be nobody there to ask. So I tried to make him think.

"My ma gave me this beautiful gold watch. It's sittin' in a box at the bank. I never wear it. Why?"

"You don't like it?"

"Nope. If I could, I'd wear the thing every day. Why don't I?"

I could see him try, but the answer just wouldn't come to him. I hoped whoever he had to front for him was smarter than he was.

"Don't know," he said at last.

"I run a tavern in a shitty neighborhood. If I wore it, people'd start thinking I got money. That happens, either I get robbed or audited. Either way, I get ripped off. Skim, but don't make it show. Don't make people wonder. The less they think about you the better."

I wanted to get out of there. On Sundays, the bar didn't open up again until noon. It was the one morning I didn't have to wait for Donald, so I was ready to go home. Fatboy tried to ask more questions, but I really didn't want him looking over my shoulder when I put the books back in the coal chute. We'd become friends, and I'd trusted him enough to give him a set of bar keys, but when it came to the money, I didn't trust anybody. "Gotta finish. Go home," I said.

"I wanna take my cut home."

"Your cut."

"The currency exchange."

I took a deep breath. "It's late. Bad neighborhood. You should do it another time."

"Where is it?" His voice spiked. "It's not where you put it."

"What, you came down here lookin' for it?"

He glared at me. "It's my money, Andy."

"I had to move it to keep it safe. Don't worry about it. I'll give it to your front man, when I meet him. Now go home. I gotta finish."

He didn't say anything, but his nostrils flared. I thought about old man Krause and the hammer, and all those news stories about Gacy killing kids and burying them in the crawlspace. I realized I'd left the .38s upstairs. A chill passed through me.

I took a deep breath. "It's safe, I swear. You'll get it when you need it." I patted him on the back. "Now go home. I gotta finish."

He walked up the stairs slowly, like he was thinking long and hard about something. I stood there and stared at the back of his legs and waited for him to turn around. But he just kept going, and soon his shoes were out of sight. When I heard the door click shut, I finally breathed.

I put the ledgers away and checked that our bundles were all still there in the coal chute. I had to reach through the black dust and put my hands on them, and that wasn't enough, so I had to take them out and feel them heavy in my hands, and that still wasn't enough, so I had to open them and thumb through them really quick, dirty hands on green money. Finally I put them away, farther back than before.

I went back upstairs. I remember wondering if Fatboy was up there in the bar waiting for me, and wishing I had the .38 in my pocket, but the place was empty as death. I double-checked that we'd done everything. I grabbed the register gun and slipped it into my pocket. Then I walked out the door and locked up.

I remember the sidewalk covered with packed snow. I remember the icy wind tearing through my pants and shirt. I remember that the only sounds were the hum of the streetlights and the click of the stoplight. I remember keys dropping through my numb fingers, and wondering if I'd ever get through a day when it didn't happen. I remember slipping the key into the lock.

I remember the sound of shoes crunching snow.

Pop. Before I could turn around, the first bullet slammed my skull. *Pop.* The second sent me to the pavement. I knew I was going down, but I couldn't stop myself. I couldn't even put my hands in front of me. My head slammed against the door and my legs gave way.

Hands reached into my pockets and took my wallet, cash, pistol, and keys. Shoes crunched snow. Car pulled up. Door opened. Door closed. Car pulled away.

I couldn't look up. My head wouldn't let me. The only thing I could do was watch my blood melt the snow. I don't know how long it was, but the next thing I remembered was the sound of sirens, and fingers pressing against my throat.

Spike Ass

I was in St. Anne's ICU.

Just outside the door, there was a state trooper. A guy from the State's Attorney's office stood next to the bed. He looked like somebody'd shoved a spike up his ass. He was tall, pale, and thin. He wore this grey suit with a tie so tight his neck veins popped. He was carrying a stack of photos.

"You're lucky," Spike Ass said. "Head shot grazed your skull. Who'd you piss off?"

"Don't know." I said. And I didn't. Or there were too many people to narrow it down. It could've been Fatboy. It could've been the Reverend, coming out of hiding to cut ties and clean things up. It could've been the Outfit, on account of the currency exchange. It could have been some drunk I'd banned. Hell, it could have been somebody looking for quick cash. That's what it had become. Even if you were like me, even if you were careful, even if you played it straight, it was out there waiting for you.

Spike Ass pushed a table over to my bed. One by one, he put the photos on it. You'd have thought the whole neighborhood bought stuff out of that garage. An old man loaded a TV into his station wagon. A lady and her kid walked down the alley wearing coats with the tags still on them. Catholic school girls stood at the garage door with dresses over their arms. A guy and his wife pushed a fucking washing machine on a dolly. I thought they had it all, but there was one picture missing. The safe. They'd missed the currency exchange.

"Take advantage of your luck," Spike Ass said. "You might get off. We don't want you. We want cops. Your friend, Jerry. And his old partner. If you don't take the deal, we'll offer it to the junkie. He doesn't want to go back. He'll jump at it."

I just lay there and stared.

Some quick background: I'd decided to become a burglar at the same time the State's Attorney had decided he wanted to be mayor. He'd jumped ship to the Republicans so he could go head-to-head with the Machine. But he'd needed a big case, a heater. A case that would give him his chance to shove his face in the trough.

Somewhere in there, the State's Attorney heard rumors about a commander on the West Side shaking down taverns. That's when he borrowed Spike Ass from the state police.

Spike Ass, the guy laying down the pictures, had a real name: Paul Pajeski. He wasn't just honest. He was famous for being honest. Typical dumb Pollack, trying to be straight in a crooked city. But that was the one thing I hadn't expected: running into an honest cop.

I wasn't the only one who knew what a rarity that was. Hell, back when he was a Chicago cop, the Trib was doing stories on him. Back then, before his bosses knew what a pain in the ass he was going to be, he'd been stationed downtown. The asshole went around City Hall giving out parking tickets to all the gangsters and politicians. A guy from the mayor's office told him to stop, but he kept on stuffing the tickets under windshield wipers. Pajeski got suspended.

But somebody called the Trib. They put the story on page three. So many letters and phone calls poured into the mayor's office that something had to be done. Pajeski got un-suspended, and the mayor himself gave him a commendation. Then, as soon as they could, his bosses transferred the bastard out to O'Hare where he couldn't do any more damage.

But Spike Ass found a way. One day, during rush hour, he stopped a limo speeding down the berm. It turned out to be a North Side congressman. The congressman pulled the old do-you-know-who-I-am thing, but Pajeski insisted on giving him a bunch of tickets. The more the congressman bitched, the more violations Spike Ass wrote. Finally the congressman lost his shit, got out of the limo, and started poking his finger in the cop's chest. Pajeski grabbed that finger and bent it back until the congressman was on his knees. Spike Ass put him in handcuffs.

This time Spike Ass not only made the papers, he made it to TV.

The congressman had to go on TV himself and apologize. He tried his best to look like a TV dad. He wore a sweater and sat in his living room with his wife, kids, and dog around him. He looked right into the camera and said that he'd made a mistake and that no man was above the law, including him. He praised Spike Ass for being so honest, and asked for forgiveness for being so rude.

It was bullshit. The Machine knew they couldn't get rid of Pajeski, but after that, they made damn sure he knew he was never going to get promoted.

But Spike Ass got the last word. He joined the state troopers, where I guess everybody's honest, because he'd made goddamn inspector by the time he was showing me those fucking pictures.

I thought about all this as I lay there and stared.

Spike Ass went on: "We know about you and Rita. Your friend spends money on a stripper while his wife can't pay bills. He's an asshole and doesn't give a shit. We'll put him away. We'll move you. Nice little apartment somewhere downstate. She'll go with. It'd be helluva lot better for you, her, and her kids. A new life."

That was his play. Hope. He put it on a stick and dangled it in front of me. He thought I'd be a good dog, sit up, and give up everybody.

I gotta admit, it was tempting.

But what Spike Ass didn't know was that I was running out of hope and there could never really be a new life for me. No matter where they moved me, I would end up a drooling piece of meat. And, when that happened, they'd put me in some shit hole. I was fucked, unless I had the money.

Spike Ass thought I'd be easy. If he'd caught me just a few weeks earlier, he'd have been right. But lying in that bed, I knew that, even though my lungs filled, my heart pumped, and my muscles twitched, I was dead. He could do nothing for me.

"You can shove your deal up your ass," I said.

"Huh?" He just stood there confused.

"Shove. Your. Fucking. Deal. Up. Your. Fucking. Ass. That's all I've got to say to you."

Pajeski's neck veins twitched and his temples throbbed, but he kept his cool. "I think you're gonna have a lot more to say pretty soon."

I shook my bandaged head, just a little. "I'm not sayin' shit else without my lawyer present."

Spike Ass looked confused. Like a school kid, he'd probably practiced his pitch for hours, memorizing every line. I liked that look on his face. I liked making him fail.

"Hurry up, motherfucker," I said. "Ain't got all day."

◇◇◇

But it didn't go that way.

In Chicago, with enough money, you can beat a murder charge. A burglary rap should have been a breeze. But with the State's Attorney hot for me, it was another story. The mayor knew that, if he wanted to keep bleeding the public, he had to make sure this was handled right. Everything had to be done clean.

We made the papers and TV. And my lawyer laid it out clear to me: the impossible had happened. There was nobody to bribe. We could've walked into the courthouse waving fistfuls of cash, and everybody'd have run like I was handing out the clap.

But I could still fight.

When you know you're dead, fear disappears. Nothing gets in the way. It's like walking into a clearing. If I'd have pled guilty, the bar license would have been worthless. As it was, I wasn't going to get shit for the place, but something was better than nothing. And there was always the currency exchange money.

A week or so later, when my skull felt okay, I had my lawyer post bail. Because I had no priors, I had enough to pay it.

I got out and went straight to the bar.

Before I even walked through the door, I was hit by the smell of stale beer.

When I opened up and switched on the lights, I saw that they'd ripped the place apart. There was broken glass everywhere. They'd torn gashes in the stools and booths, and thrown the stuffing all over the floor. They'd emptied the coolers and dropped the bottles. They'd opened the taps and let them run. Puddles of beer were everywhere. The register was unplugged and the drawer ripped out. Cash and coins were scattered all over the back bar. The TV was lying on top of a radiator with its back ripped off. The jukebox was pulled away from the wall, and they'd ripped the felt off of the pool table.

It didn't surprise me. They'd searched everybody's house. They were just more gung ho when it came to me. Spike Ass didn't like being called a motherfucker.

Then I remembered the basement, and suddenly everything upstairs meant nothing.

I dashed down there. The basement was a mess, too. There were heaps of boxes and broken glass, and a mush of chips and beer on the floor. There were chunks of concrete and dirt where the safe had been.

The coal chute door was open. I didn't bother with the gloves. I put my hands into the mound of coal dust. The second set of books was gone. I got a stool and put my head inside the chute. I reached further in, way in the back.

I only started breathing again when I felt the plastic bags.

I put the bags on the table and wiped away the dust. In one were the two last .38s. In the other were the bundles of cash, Fatboy's and mine. I thanked God for lazy cops, shoved the bags even further into the pile, and shut the door.

When I climbed the stairs, Railroad Bob was sitting on a ripped stool, smoking a cigarette. I'd forgotten to lock the door behind me. He looked at me, threw a five on the bar, and said, "Old Style, gherkin."

I was tired and wanted to sleep. I thought about kicking him out, but I was still in the bar business and he was a regular. I opened a bottle of Old Style, threw it on the bar, took his money, and gave him his change. Then I stocked the coolers and started cleaning up.

Making Plans

It was a Friday night, a week after I'd gotten out. Besides me, it was the Skeletons, Gin and Tonic Doc, and Railroad Bob. We were in our usual places: Railroad Bob in his booth, the Skeletons on their stools, and Doc in the perfect spot to pick up rough trade. I stood behind the bar. The coolers and ice bins were full. The register held plenty of singles and quarters.

But I knew no one else would come through the door. Maybe an old man wandering in for a to-go-six pack. It'd been like that for days.

The state cops had a car parked across the street taking pictures of anybody that even came close to the bar. I'd complained to my lawyer, but he'd said I'd already pissed them off enough, and that I should let it go if I didn't want more trouble.

"When we win, we'll sue the bastards," he'd said.

"Whattya mean *we*?" I'd asked. "When *we* lose, you goin' to prison with me?"

He'd told me to stay positive, but of course, it was all bullshit. Lawyers have to give you something to hold on to while they lift your wallet. Whoever'd taken a shot at me hadn't come back since the state investigators had started hanging around. That was the only positive I could think of.

But others were staying away, too. Rita refused to see me. She wouldn't even talk to me over the phone. As for the bar, none of the Chicago cops could take the chance of coming in. And to make it worse, Zenith had cut their night shift and laid off at least ten percent of the rest of the workers. That night, when it hit midnight and even the St. Anne's nurses didn't come in, I decided there was no point in staying open.

I locked the door, but I didn't want to be alone. I threw quarters into the jukebox and I bought drinks. Finally, when I'd put his fifth gin and tonic in front of him, Doc put his hand up and said, "Enough."

"Enough what?"

"You always struck me as a smart guy, Andy. How'd you get caught up in all this?"

It all came out of me. I told him about the Huntington's and the burglaries and how all my plans had fallen apart.

He let me ramble for a while. He nodded along, until finally, he put a finger up and stood. He took off his suit coat. Under the bar lights, I could see through his shirt. There were tattoos of what looked like ropes. Then he unbuttoned his shirt and, as he did, I saw that what I thought were ropes were vines, and, as he pulled the shirt off, those vines ended in roses that looked so real I thought that, if I'd tried, I could've plucked them from his skin. And as the vines moved up his shoulders, there were shades of green, like the sun was moving across them, and the red of the roses did the same. The petals looked like a light wind could blow them from his arms.

I'd never seen anything like it.

"No one does this here," he said. "It's Japanese. I spent the last ten years learning how. There's a parlor on South State where I rent space. We get soldiers, sailors and teenagers. And no roses. Nothing like this. They get tattoos of women with big tits, hearts with bloody daggers, snakes, dragons, and, of course, tigers. If I have to draw one more fucking tiger, I'll go insane. But the parlor does have its benefits. There's a back room and occasionally there's a young man who wants more than a tattoo."

I'm sure I made a face.

"This sort of thing offends you?" He buttoned his shirt.

"Growing up in my neighborhood, you could be a thief and a liar," I said. "You could beat your kids and cheat on your wife. You could even kill somebody. But you couldn't be a faggot."

"Your neighborhood has issues."

I smirked. "It's your neighborhood too!"

"No. I live up north. Teach English at a Catholic university on the North Side. I have a PhD in literature."

"So Doc is…"

"Not just a nickname," he smiled. "That's why I come down here. The Catholic clergy hates a cocksucker unless they're the ones doing the sucking."

"Nobody up there knows?"

"You know how things are. As long as you keep up appearances, nobody says anything. When I first started teaching, I wrote a novel about an affair between and older and younger man. It was good. Really good. But to get it published, I had to change them into a straight couple. Ruined it. Made it second rate. I was supposed to be a writer. Instead, I'm just some old queer. I teach books to people who don't read them, and I draw tigers instead of roses. We all make plans, but they usually come to nothing."

Doc had been coming in for years, but I realized just then how little I knew about him. I wondered why I'd never bothered to ask. I should've asked.

"I know you're probably going to have to close the place," he went on. "We'll probably lose touch." He put his coat back on. "You've been good to me."

He tried to buy a six pack. I threw it in a bag and gave him back his money. He thanked me and then turned to Railroad Bob. "Bob. How about a bubble bath and blowjob?"

Bob pulled himself up, scratched his head, and said, "Lead on, gherkin."

Doc tucked the six pack under his arm and helped Bob from his booth. Bob leaned on Doc as they walked to the door. When they opened it, Bob raised his arm toward the cops, gave them the finger, and hollered: "Behold, fuckers! Something wicked this way comes."

I locked the door behind them, went out to the garage, and grabbed an old shopping cart. I filled it with top-shelf bottles, premium stuff from the back bar. I pushed it back up front and told the Skeletons I was closing early. They were both pissed until I told them the shopping cart was theirs.

I showed them out the back. The old lady pushed the cart through the door. Before the old man went through, I tugged at his coat. I handed him a .38. He slipped it into his pocket.

"Thanks," he said.

"Careful," I said.

And as the old bastards walked down the alley pushing that cart and bickering, I thought of how much I'd miss them. I lowered the garage door and locked it. For the first time in my life, I wasn't in the bar business.

To undercut prices in the United States, Japanese television manufacturers sold their products at inflated prices to Japanese consumers. To further reduce competition, they paid US retailers illegal rebates.

- Pat Choate, Agents of Influence: How Japan Manipulates America's Political and Economic System

The Quality of a Name

When you're a thief, especially if you have a friend like Jerry, there's a very good chance everything will go to shit. You have to be prepared.

It's easy to become somebody else. If you've got a thousand dollars, there is a lawyer who will hand you the birth certificate, social security card, and utility bills of a recently deceased person. You can take them downtown and tell a bored clerk that you've lost your driver's license. That clerk will pretend to look at the birth certificate and utility bills. She'll take your money. Another clerk will snap your picture and hand you a license. With that license and the social security card, you'll get a passport. You can go on disability and get Medicare. You can find a nice warm place to die.

The next day, the next-to-last day, I went back to the bar. I had one last thing to do.

I put thread, needles, grease pencil, and a knife and on the bar. I turned the parka inside out and spread it out onto one of the tables. I took the knife and carefully cut out the lining and pulled fistfuls of the stuffing from the coat. I put the coat and stuffing to the side and laid the lining out on the table. Then I took the grease pencil and slowly traced the pattern onto the table. I put it to one side.

I carefully laid out a layer of cash within the pattern. Then, one by one, I sewed the bills together. When I had one layer done, I went onto the next. I kept it up until it was a thick layer of green. I laid stuffing on top of the lining. Then I put the money on top of it and sandwiched it in with more stuffing. I sewed the lining back into the parka.

I put a thick wad of cash in my pocket, put the coat on, put the last .38 in my pocket, and walked to the back door. I opened it, stepped out, locked up, and went down the alley. I was still a little worried that the Reverend was gonna come back to clean everything up, so I kept my eyes open, but I didn't hurry. I didn't have to. An envelope had been passed.

I zigzagged through backyards, snow-clogged alleys, and icy gangways until I reached the Austin Boulevard viaduct. It ran parallel to Central and under the train tracks. I started to walk through it, but, after a few feet, I stopped and looked back to make sure I wasn't being followed. Then I started again, picking up the pace so I wouldn't miss shift change.

I knew it would all be OK once I told her about the money. We'd grab her kids and run. At least for a little while, she wouldn't have to plead with some bastard to not shut off the gas, or beg some suit to wait a day before cashing her mortgage payment, or ask the nun for more time for the tuition, or ask some boss for more hours at a job she hated. Best of all, she wouldn't have to put up with the looks from the fucking people who'd never had to do any of it.

I kept walking. Chunks of concrete were missing from the viaduct pillars. You could see the rebar. It felt like any minute the thing would come down on my head. On the white walls, somebody'd scrawled **Almighty Freaks** in huge letters. Halfway through, a patch of ice covered the sidewalk. There was no way around. I tried to jump it, but didn't make it. My feet went out from under me and I landed hard on my elbow.

Where the viaduct ended, the Zenith plant began. There were a lot of buildings, all two stories and red brick. They went on for blocks. On the roof, above everything, was a grey water tower with **ZENITH** painted on it. Where there wasn't brick, there were sections of little frosted windows covered with iron mesh and bars. At the center of everything were two large glass doors. Above it, the company's slogan had been painted on the brick in big white letters: **Zenith – The Quality Goes in Before the Name Goes On.** That's where I waited for her.

When shift change came, they filed out. At first, there was a steady flow, but, after a few minutes, it wound down to a trickle. I thought I'd missed her, or that she hadn't gone to work that day, but then she came out. Her hands were stuffed in her coat pockets and her head was down. She passed without seeing me. I called after her. She stopped, turned, and looked. At first her eyes got wide, but then they became slits.

"Fuck off," she said.

She turned and started walking again, but quicker this time. I followed her, but I couldn't keep up. I called after her, but she kept going. Finally, I yelled, "I can help."

She stopped and laughed. Then she turned, looked at me, and said: "You can't. Nobody can."

"What's going on?"

"My brother talked. He took the fuckin' deal. Once he testifies, they're going to give him probation and move him."

"That's good."

"That's good?" She erupted. "I'll never see my brother again! My kids will never see their uncle. What's so fucking *good* about that? Because he's not going back to prison? I was supposed to help him. You were too. All we did was fuck him up. That's all we ever do. And Jerry's in fucking jail!"

I breathed hard. "I didn't know that."

"Of course you didn't," she said. "Since they talked to you in the hospital, he's been in jail. Called me collect from a phone on the deck. They're tryin' to put the squeeze on him, too. Fuckin' Jerry won't give up anybody. Hell, even the fucking commander gave up somebody, but not Jerry. Loyal to his friends to the goddamn end, except to me and his kids. He knows about you and me. They used it to try and get to him. They told him that, while he was in there, his best friend would be fucking his wife. But he still wouldn't rat. So they're gonna make an example of him. He's gonna do ten years. He's pissed off at me. Aint that a kick in the ass? The bastard's been cheating on me for years and *he's* pissed at *me*."

"I'm sorry," I started. "Look, we can…"

"We can what? My kids are getting shit on at school. The neighbors are being assholes. All I've got are bills. My dad won't help me, and, like everybody else, I'm gonna lose my job. I was gonna front a bar for my brother, but that's fucked too. So, I've got nothing. But, one way or another, I'm gonna get my kids out of here."

I took another deep breath of icy air. "We can do that."

She shook her head. "If I could, I'd get them away from me too."

"You're crazy. The kids are lucky to have you."

She looked at me like I'd said the world was flat. "We're fuckups," she said. "This place makes you like that."

"Not you."

She came closer, unzipped my coat, put her arms around me, and I felt the familiar rush.

"Your coat's all sewn up funny," she said.

"Money from the currency exchange." I smiled. "I'm bundled up."

But then her hands moved from my back to my belly. She was feeling for a wire. There was no one left for her to trust. She waited until the street was just about empty before she pulled her hands away. Then she took a step back.

"Andy, you walk around thinking you're so smart, but, honest to God, you can be so stupid. I'm a great big goddamn fuckup just like you. You're acting like you're gonna save me from this shit? This whole fucking thing was my idea."

All my life, I'd told myself that the world was made up of liars, thieves, and hustlers, but that once in a while, if you lucked out, you'd run into somebody who'd be straight with you. I thought it was her. In that street, she slapped me out of it. Hell, she was a better hustler than many I'd known. Of course she was, she was one of us. Why did I ever expect her to be any different?

But all that didn't matter. "Let's leave," I said. "I've got the cash. We can go wherever we want."

"Like where?"

I shrugged. "Florida? Get out of this fuckin' cold, somewhere."

"What about my kids?"

"Bring 'em."

She blew into her hands and shivered. I took a step and wrapped my arms around her. We stood that way for a minute, and then she pushed me away. "They'll get us caught."

"Leave 'em with your dad. In a few years, you'll come back."

A wave of sadness came over her face. "Can't."

I took the wad of cash from my pocket. I put half of it in her hand.

"Drop your kids off in the morning with your dad. Give him the cash. We can send him more from the road."

"Andy, I..."

"We can do this. It's gotta be this way." I told her the address of a motel on Mannheim. I told her I'd meet her in the coffee shop at noon. I told her I loved her. I told her I needed her. I said anything I had to. Because even though I'd spouted all that shit about how it didn't matter what happened because I was already dead, I was still me: a selfish little prick who wanted what he wanted. Hell, I even got a few tears to roll down my face.

"Please," I said. She put the cash in her pocket, nodded, and walked away. When she was out of sight, I walked to a used car lot on Grand.

Mannheim Road

Everything on Mannheim was concrete, steel, plate glass and tar. From the Eisenhower to the Kennedy, it was nothing but motels, strip clubs, bars, car rental places, and gas stations. Day and night, there was a steady flow of traffic.

I waited for that cab for hours. Sometimes I'd see one and I'd jump out of the booth, but then it'd pass and I'd sit back down. I tried calling her from the payphone by the front door, but no one picked up. I called her father. He said he hadn't seen her.

When it got dark, I gave up. I paid and walked to the car. I hated her for not coming with me. I hated her kids for keeping her from me. I hated my parents for leaving me with nothing but years of drunks. I hated that I'd been so practical all those years ago when I'd stood in that basement, telling her we needed to face reality. Reality? Reality put me where I was. Fuck reality.

I put the key in the car door lock. Just as I turned it, I felt the muzzle against my skull.

She'd lied. He was out on bail. Or she hadn't lied, and he'd gotten out.

I tried to turn and look at him.

"Stay still, motherfucker," Jerry said. "Unzip the coat. Slowly! And let it drop."

I did. It was cold. I shivered. A blanket of goosebumps spread over my arms. There was the swoosh of the traffic. There was the buzz of the neon. The hammer clicked back.

Maybe he'd made her tell him where I was going to be. Or maybe she'd thought he was just going to talk to me about the money. Or maybe she knew.

But all that didn't matter.

And maybe he hadn't planned on doing it, but somewhere between what he'd planned and the click of the hammer, he'd realized the truth. If she'd have let me, I'd have taken her from him, even if that meant taking his kids too. And, no matter how much he said he wanted to leave them, they were his family. It was the one thing he couldn't let anybody steal.

"Jerry," I said.

"No," he said.

In the movies, when somebody gets killed, the victim usually gets to relive a laundry list of memories. Everything slows down. The hammer hits. There's a flash that lights up the victim's face. The bullet crawls from the muzzle. It slowly crashes into the skull. Tiny chips of bone fly. A V of fluid sprays.

But standing in that parking lot, when my friend pulled the trigger, I found out that's not what happens.

In the split-second after the *pop*, you only have time for one memory.

Mine was the look on her face when she opened the door and was happy to see it was me.

About the Author

Bob Hartley was raised on the West Side of Chicago. He holds an MFA in fiction from the University of Pittsburgh. His first novel, *Following Tommy*, was published in 2012 by Cervena Barva Press to extremely favorable reviews. He has been, among other things, a writer, actor, singer, teacher, bartender, mailroom clerk, and washer of soap molds. He currently makes his living as a respiratory therapist and lives in Pittsburgh with his wife and two children.

About Tortoise Books

Slow and steady wins in the end, even in the publishing industry. Tortoise Books is dedicated to finding and promoting quality authors who haven't yet found a niche in the marketplace—writers producing memorable and engaging works that will stand the test of time.

Learn more at www.tortoisebooks.com.